PRAISE FOR BE

TALK TILL T
RUN OUT

Won...

2nd Place Ethel Rohan Novel Excerpt Award in the 2019 South-Making Keats Literary Competition

More acclaim...

"Novelist Benedicte Grima has taken an under-represented world she knows well from her own work over several decades as folklorist and ethnographer and offered up the reader a rare and stunning glimpse of those islands of immigrants who survive abroad while not assimilating to their foreign surroundings. Seen through the eyes of the well-meaning, bumbling, unprepared and deeply culturally-entrenched family patriarch, Nur Ali, this tough and rare glimpse into little understood lives—even by the people living them, is an important story for our times and should be read by anyone who wants to understand more deeply what it means to belong in our vastly interconnected world."

– Beebe Bahrami, Anthropologist & Author of *The Spiritual Traveler*; *Café Oc*; *Café Neanderthal*; *Camino de Santiago.*

"Grima, one of America's few Pukhtun scholars and an extremely keen observer of Pukhtun culture, both in its homeland and the diaspora, follows an ordinary Pukhtun family as it survives in its native area, beleaguered by Taliban and the Pakistani military, and as some of its members seek fortunes but not assimilation in places as far away as America. The story ends with their cultural identity intact but their aspirations defeated in many ways by the modern, post 9/11 world."

– John Dixon, Former Diplomat in Pakistan

"This bittersweet story of hardscrabble migration and exile in the west simultaneously tracks another story, that of a Pashtun homeland, the Swat Valley in Pakistan, transformed by political chaos, religious militancy, and economic dislocation. While Malala Yousafzai survived such trauma and flourished at Oxford, Grima reminds us that "Exit-West" journeys have had complex outcomes for individuals of particular ages, educations, genders, kinship relations, and cultures. This is a tale of sacrifice, duty, and love. It follows a personal struggle to preserve a customary home and family relations amidst the alienations and dislocations of a world transformed by the twenty-first century."

– Robert Nichols, Stockton University, Author of *A History of Pashtun Migration 1775-2006*

"No Westerner knows Pakistan's Swat Valley better than Benedicte Grima. Her novel of exile and multi-sided peril is a triumph of ethnographic insight. We learn not only of the Pashtun people in Swat but also of their immigrant culture in America and, painfully, of America's treatment of them."

– Whitney Azoy, Anthropologist and former diplomat, Middle East Institute. Author of *Buzkashi, Game of Power in Afghanistan.*

AN IMMIGRANT'S TALE AT 7-ELEVEN

talk
till the minutes run out

Benedicte Grima

HigherLife Development Services, Inc.

PO Box 623307

Oviedo, Florida 32762

(407) 563-4806

www.ahigherlife.com

ISBN: 978-1-7332289-8-5 (paperback)

ISBN: 978-1-7332289-9-2 (ebook)

Printed in the United States of America

10 9 8 7 6 5 4 3 2 1

Library of Congress Cataloging-in-Publication Data

To Paul, whose love and patience allowed me to rekindle the passion for writing I had let die over the decades. To Leilani, whose sophisticated reading of the first version opened my eyes to the difference between social science and fiction writing. To Colleen, whose tech and marketing skills helped me face the dreaded public world and create a platform. And to Beebe, whose punctilious editing rounded and perfected the telling. I couldn't have done this without each of your contributions.

INTRODUCTION

The ability to see both sides of a story is a curse.

I like to think that what I present here is the other side of our perception of immigrants. Particularly in conversations with his wife or with other exiles at the mosque, the aging exile of this story, Nur Ali, conveys America and non-Muslims as he sees and experiences them from his inner-city 7-Eleven. It should not be read as an insult on American culture but as a map to understand why others perceive us the way they do.

This is a work of fiction. Although based on ethnographic fieldwork conducted over ten years in Pakistan's Swat Valley, and another ten years embedded in the Pashtun exile community in the US, the names and characters are either the product of the author's imagination or are used fictitiously, and any resemblance to actual persons, living or dead, is entirely coincidental.

PROLOGUE: THE EXILES

We encounter this underworld of unauthorized immigrants daily in our busy lives: cab drivers, convenience store and fast food employees, gas station attendants, food truck servers, cleaning staff, and farm laborers. We just don't stop to ask their stories. They are often too busy on their phones talking with family back home or furiously exchanging news about their exile community, warning each other of raids and deportations, like stalked prey, ever on the lookout for the hawk.

At a time when sparks are flying over building walls and immigration policy, and bias has infiltrated our political and cultural environment to the disadvantage of outsiders, it is now time to consider the other side of immigration. The "melting pot" theory used to be the standard, and immigrants flocked to assimilate and create a homogenous society based on language, culture, and a fervent belief that America was the place to flourish.

A plethora of immigrant literature surfaced, success stories with firsthand accounts of immigrants who struggled to achieve assimilation into American society. Education and a strong work ethic were the keys to rising above and "making it." First generation immigrants ensured their children became fully Americanized—language, sports, jobs, friends—sometimes at the expense of their original cultural heritage.

But 9/11 brought this to a halt. Suddenly all Muslims became the enemy, all were assumed to be associated with al-Qaeda, the Taliban, and terrorism in general. There is no need to repeat the stories we've all read of violent acts performed against Muslims for no other reason than bias. "All

Muslims are terrorists," the FBI was found teaching its trainees in 2009. The more it could identify, round up, and deport potential terrorists, the more efficient the government could appear in keeping the nation secure.

The blatant xenophobia demonstrated in the US government has spurred a different group of temporary unauthorized immigrants who harbor no desire to assimilate in any manner, who are fully aware they can never flourish in America. They settle wherever their ethnic group has already established permanency. They live as cheaply as possible, hustle to work for cash in whatever manner they can, often balancing multiple jobs, and send as much of that cash home to support their family. They know they are disadvantaged and unprivileged economically, but they accept this to maintain anonymity and remain under the government's radar. In many cases, they earn more than what they could be earning back home, often under oppressive conditions. They rely on the exiled group's in-house resources: doctors, lawyers, and service specialists. Nothing can persuade them to turn to local authorities for advice or assistance. On the contrary, they are forever looking over their shoulder for these authorities; they live in fear of deportation. Apart from laboring to send money home, they aspire only to quietly and anonymously live out their term and then return to retire.

PROLOGUE: SWAT

There is a valley in northern Pakistan, in the foothills of the Hindu Kush mountain range, called Swat Valley. The valley follows the Swat River, which winds down to the southern plains, where it merges with the Indus River. The northernmost part of Swat, less inhabited than the flatter southern portion, is narrow and mountainous, spotted with few villages. The mountains climb on either side of the river, and although the villiages are carved into narrow terraces for agriculture and homes built in steps, there is only so much livable area.

By 2005 the Pakistani Taliban, made up of Pashtuns and other ethnic groups from all over Pakistan and Afghanistan, as well as other Muslim nations, had taken over the Swat Valley as their center of operations and recruitment. The Taliban at first tended to settle and find acceptance in rural Pashtun areas because they sought to implement rules and a way of life which already existed and was found acceptable there. Swat Pashtuns kept strict segregation rules, for example, which the Taliban reinforced, although the latter took it a step further in preventing girls from attending school other than in-home Quranic recitations. Women were still publicly stoned in Swat as punishment for alleged infidelity, and the Taliban reinforced that. But the Taliban encountered resistance in matters where Swat Pashtuns prioritized their own culture over Islam, as with their practice of wailing laments at wakes and funerals despite the Taliban mullahs' efforts to ban the practice. And the local population did not appreciate that the bazaars and buses, once abuzz with sounds of recorded music, had been silenced by the Taliban's ban on such things.

By 2009, Pakistan sent its military into Swat to retake control from the Taliban. Many Swatis, including Nur Ali, the main character of this story and his family, despised the Taliban, who disrupted their agrarian lifestyle and interfered with their independence. With his father's vigor, he and his family labeled them hypocrites. But they equally despised the Pakistan Military who abused their power in attempting to identify Taliban sympathizers. These soldiers fought hard to counter the Taliban infiltration and takeover of such rural areas, but their aggressive efforts met with as much resistance as the Taliban's in Swat.

The army launched military attacks on villages to eliminate the Taliban from the area. This process included numerous and continued home invasions to locate and arrest Taliban members and sympathizers. Village locals in Swat like Nur Ali fostered an intense dislike for both the Taliban and the government, both of whom threatened the self-sufficient agrarian lifestyle and culture that flourished in Swat.

Nur Ali's son, Iqbal, along with his friends, had participated in a local rally in Mardan to protest the government, at which they had hurled rocks at the soldiers. Iqbal's rock, as luck would have it, hit a soldier hard enough between the eyes to kill him instantly. Iqbal managed to get away, but he had been identified and incorrectly labeled by the government as a Taliban sympathizer, and they were now in pursuit.

The US supported Pakistan's efforts to restrict the Taliban and looked for suspicious signs of backing in things like immigrants from Swat sending money home, especially if the Pakistani government suggested that these people were affiliated with the Taliban. Every time the American authorities could single out and deport someone suspected of terrorism, and publicize it in the national media, they boosted public credibility in their efforts to protect national security. Nur Ali, who had left long before 9/11 and the Taliban invasion of Swat, believed he and his entire family were wanted by the Pakistan government because of Iqbal's actions. As a result, the US and ICE in particular, were on his trail, suspecting that he was sending money for Taliban support. It was a case of "any friend of my enemy is my enemy," as well as mislabeling people and then passing on the stereotype.

Both to avoid the Taliban and the army, and to seek jobs and incomes nonexistent in northern Swat, many males aged nineteen to forty fled for various destinations from local mountain hamlets to larger cities in Pakistan or to the Gulf: Kuwait, Dubai, Abu Dhabi, or Qatar. Those who remained took part in local militant armies whose goal was to protect and defend civilians who remained in the villages from both the army and the Bearded Ones, as the Taliban had become known in Swat. Today, still, the Swat Valley is controlled by the Pakistan Army and remains closed to foreigners without military permits.

To complicate the existence of residents remaining, in 2010 torrential rains produced massive flooding and landslides that devastated the Swat Valley.

It is from the Swat Valley that comes Nur Ali, an illegal immigrant, wrongly accused of supporting the Taliban and pursued by U.S. authorities. He is one of those many faces we see daily in food carts, taxis, convenience stores, fried chicken eateries, and gas stations and know little about.

This story takes place between 2009 and 2011.

WHO'S WHO?

Ali, Nur: Main character. Middle-aged man from Khwaza Khel, Swat, Pakistan. Head of family. AKA Qaidada by his family, and Mama by other exiled Pashtuns. Employee at 7-Eleven.

Shahgofta: Nur Ali's wife, in Pakistan, AKA Bibi, used to address mothers and older women

Nur Ali's Siblings and Cousins:

Mahmad Ali: Brother, married to *Sabina.*

Yusuf Ali: Brother, married to *Lawangina.*

Sardar Ali: Brother, married to *Salma.*

Naheela: Sister, married to *Amanullah.*

Na'im: Maternal cousin.

Children of Nur Ali and Shahgofta:

Ahmad: Oldest son, married to *Rabia.*

Iqbal: Second son, married to *Sher Banu.*

Naser: Youngest son.

Shahgul: Daughter, married to *Liaqat Ali.*

Naseema: Youngest daughter.

Nazia: Granddaughter

Aftab: Grandson

Nur Ali's Co-Workers at the 7-Eleven:

Layla: Young woman from Morocco, day time assistant manager.

Michael: Christian Pashto speaker from Peshawar.

Mo: Young man from Morocco.

Momen Khan: Store franchisee, from Afghanistan.

Samuel: Christian Pakistani.

Shiriney: Store franchisee. Wife of Momen Khan.

Sherry: Elderly woman from the same street as the store.

Adam: Son of franchisees.

Friends and Acquaintances in the Local Exiled Pashtun Community

Bacha Gul: From Madyan, Swat. 7-Eleven, at another location.

Mir Zaman: Charsadda, Swat. Cab driver.

Kashef: Topi, Swat. Cab driver.

Rahim Jan: Imam Derrai, Swat.

Adam: Son of store franchisees, Momen Khan and Shiriney

Moambar: Imam Derrai, Swat.

Matthew: Christian Pashto speaker from Peshawar. A Former coworker and good friend.

7-ELEVEN

"Salam alaykum," Nur Ali greeted his friend on the phone at the 7-Eleven where he worked.

"Walaykum salam," replied Bacha Gul, from his 7-Eleven across town.

"Did you go to the mosque today?" Nur Ali spoke loudly, while annunciating clearly, wanting his friend to grasp every word. He furiously scratched his arm through the sleeve of his loose-fitting button-down shirt. "There was a new deportation story. It was an Afghan family. They've been here for years. The guy is a computer technician who travels a lot for his job and supports the family nicely. His parents are old; his kids all in school here. Well, they first suspected him of Taliban support, and after months of pursuing him and questioning the entire family, they found nothing on him. He came up clean. But because they had to justify their efforts, they cast blame on the old father who had entered some wrong information on his immigration papers, and they're sending him back. Alone and old, while his family remains here! It's inhuman!"

"Okay, I only heard in the news that the authorities had found someone they suspected and were deporting him," retorted Bacha Gul, playing off Nur Ali's agitation. "Now I understand. It seems there are more and more stories about deportations. Our people in the taxi and food truck businesses are constantly getting brought in for questioning, and everyone lives in fear these days."

"What are we supposed to do?" Nur Ali's voice was now raised and trembling, his eyes shooting flames into the telephone sitting on the counter in front of him. "We work here, mind our own business, and we are blamed for everything those rotten hypocrites who call themselves 'Muslim' do. We are insulted, hated, shunned, and now deported. When will they realize they have the wrong guys?" Instinctively, he reached his hand to rub his beard but then moved it down on his lower back, pressing where it ached and allowing himself to feel the pain there. The dull physical throbbing almost came as a relief in contrast to the sharp pangs of fear and anger that gripped his gut. He panicked that he was losing control of his life.

Bacha Gul excused himself from the conversation to deal with customers while Nur Ali lifted his gaze to the rows of cigarettes above him as if to memorize each brand and its location on the shelf, as if he cared.

PAKISTAN NOW

It was nearing four o'clock in the morning, and the night was passing by in the predictable relative calm of this hour. This was the time when things tended to slow down: The drunks and addicts had retired into states of slumber; the store robberies had occurred and been reported; the homeless and scammers who harassed night shoppers had been rounded up and carted off; and there was a lull before the morning rush. Alone now to tend the counter, he called his wife, Shahgofta, as he did each night at this time. For her, back in their village in Swat, in the compound that had housed him growing up, this hour was nearing the noon prayer time, a good time to call.

"Salam alaykum," he began, neither stating his name nor that of whom he assumed had picked up. A deep-rooted tradition of name avoidance, although it presented no thought in face-to-face encounters, did present a considerable challenge when communication was done over the phone with no visual grasp of the person on the other end. Regardless of who answered his call, Nur Ali began every conversation with a simple "Salam alaykum," as if anticipating that the person who had picked up would immediately identify his voice. And if he met with hesitation on the other end, he merely repeated "Salam alaykum," offering a second chance at voice recognition rather than his name. Occasionally, he would happen on a cousin, nephew, or distant relative who picked up the phone, and they would speak a long while before each became aware of whom they were speaking with, and this occurrence of mistaken identity always produced laughter. Of course in this instance, husband and wife knew each other's voice well.

"Walaykum salam," she answered.

"How are you?"

"All is well, God willing," she said, a standard response.

"Don't lie to me," he pressed. "I can tell by your voice that you're not feeling well." As a result of years of communicating by voice only, Nur Ali had learned to listen for and detect moods as indicated in a speaker's tone, pitch, and speed. He listened, as a blind person, for breathing, pauses, grunts and giggles to replace the look on someone's face.

"How is your headache? You know you can't hide anything from me, and that I know everything that's going on."

Perhaps Nur Ali's greatest vulnerability was his feeling of being left out of the loop, which aggravated his feelings of alienation. He was the oldest brother, and his father had been the oldest brother of his generation. That left Nur Ali as the clan leader, the head of family, the *qaida*. As such, he was supposed to know everything, especially where it concerned his own family. From his 7-Eleven, Nur Ali loved making the point of reminding family members often that he was in charge.

"Remember the time when, after talking with my ailing uncle, I teased your sister-in-law, Salma, by asking her where her sister-in-law, Sabina was, and when Salma answered that Sabina must be somewhere in the compound, I told her, 'No, she's not. She's gone out to look in on her father, who is suffering from kidney disease.' See, I know more than you all do about what's going on in your own home." He stopped talking, listening for his wife's gentle laughter, feeling satisfied that he had produced it.

Driven by this need to know all, he questioned Shahgofta and everyone else endlessly on all matters: political, social, economic, and family. To-night, he asked, "Has anyone died in the village recently?" This was so that he, armed with the information, could then call the survivors as head of family and give his condolences, a crucial gesture which lay at the heart of maintaining social relations among Pashtuns. Failure to share in joy and sorrow resulted in a sure breach of a relationship.

"Not that I know of," she replied.

"Okay, has anyone shaved their beard?" he pursued his interrogations. This particular point was of immense interest to him.

"No."

By remaining informed on social happenings in the compound, the village, and his entire family, Nur Ali could intelligently orchestrate and dictate who went where for what purpose or occasion, and if need be, escorted by whom. Shahgofta, for her part, played her role of subservient wife, reporting every visit and gift exchange, both in and out of the house, and allowed the *qaida* to dictate. But as the oldest woman of the household, and wife of the *qaida*, her selective output of information also directed what he dictated. Thus, they worked in harmony, beginning with his untiring inquisition over the phone for details on all that was happening in the family compound and beyond.

Nur Ali swore a person's health and state of mind were evident in their voice, and he didn't like the tone of hers tonight, or the slight tremble he thought he detected. It was softer than usual, almost cracked. She spoke in monosyllables and appeared to be holding back words. "I wasn't born yesterday," he told Shahgofta knowing she was ailing but trying to hide it, "I can hear you're not feeling well." And then he repeated, "I know everything about everyone. I'm Muslim, and that means I know everything about everyone." He reached back to press down on his lower back, feeling his own pain surge.

"I'm feeling better now." Shahgofta answered her husband's inquiry about her headache. She suffered from migraines, and when they came on, she tied a scarf very tightly around her head, hoping the extreme squeeze would counter the pressure inside. "I sent Naser and his cousin to the bazaar after school, and they brought me back some valium and penicillin. It's all they had today." It was common to send children on such errands. Women did not venture into the bazaar, and the adult men had for the most part fled, so Shahgofta often sent her nieces and nephews or their youngest son Naser on errands.

Placated by the pharmaceutical efficiency, Nur Ali began a new topic. "How's the situation in the village?" he asked. "There's trouble, isn't there?"

"No, everything is quiet today," Shahgofta said. "No disturbances."

"Is everyone healthy? Is everyone fasting?"

"Lawangina is unwell and can't fast for a few days. She'll have to make it up later."

Nur Ali inferred that his sister-in-law was menstruating and therefore not

12

sufficiently pure to fast.

"What are you preparing for tonight's dinner?" he asked, as he did every day of the fast, enviously picturing the special foods and missing sorely not being there.

"Potatoes and spinach. Salma is cooking lentils, and Sabina is preparing a goat meat curry with turnips."

Nur Ali recited the same litany of questions like a prayer at every call. He was also concerned, during this month of Rozha, that food and eating was all in order, and that no one was left alone to break the fast on any evening. It was so important to him and other fasting Muslims to break the fast with a special meal and in good company, as he had repeated each year growing up in the village.

"Did Naser go to school today?" Naser was their youngest child. He was conceived the last time Nur Ali was home, fifteen years ago. The *qaida* had never met his son.

"Naser walked to school with the other boys yesterday," Shahgofta reported, "but soldiers stopped and questioned them, demanding to know the names of the adult males living in their homes." Shahgofta paused, then finished, "He came home crying in fear and stayed home today, except to get me some pills."

"Those sons of dogs!" cried out Nur Ali, picking up the phone with his free hand and slamming it on the counter. "Have they no shame? It's true, what they say in the news. There is no more Islam in our country. They are completely crushing the Pashtuns and wiping us out." Holding the receiver in one hand, he scratched his arm in agitation with the fist that now throbbed from his outburst.

Nur Ali and his family despised the Taliban, who disrupted their agrarian lifestyle and interfered with their independence. With his father's vigor, he and his family had labeled them hypocrites. But they equally despised the Pakistani Army soldiers who abused their power in attempting to identify Taliban sympathizers. These soldiers fought hard to counter the Taliban infiltration and takeover of such rural areas, but their aggressive efforts met with as much resistance as the Taliban's in Swat.

"Have you heard from the boys?" Nur Ali continued scratching his forearm.

"No, nothing today," she replied. She knew he was referring to their two older sons, Ahmad and Iqbal, without mentioning their names.

With the family labeled as Taliban sympathizers, Nur Ali's older sons and two of his brothers had sought refuge from the army in an abandoned ancestral home in the higher mountains of Swat, leaving the women and children to fend for themselves in the village . Like Nur Ali, they called the house every day for an update, and occasionally hiked down for an unannounced visit to check on things. Times were hard on most people in Swat, and Nur Ali knew that he and his brother, Yusuf Ali, provided the sole support for not only his own wife and children, but his sisters-in-law and their children living in his family compound.

The political situation apart, some of Nur Ali's relatives, especially his brother Mahmad Ali, benefited from the American salary he managed to send home regularly, and they were in no hurry to interrupt the cash flow by having him come home. These individuals continued to feed his fears that he could face prosecution if he came home. Hence his hopes of return were spurred or reined in, depending with whom he spoke, sometimes he experienced both hope and dejection within the same call home. His wife and sisters-in-law reported safe conditions, while his brothers and cousins presented dangers and threats that dashed his hopes of coming home.

Nur Ali returned to the topic of that night's meal, and asked who was cooking the bread.

"Tonight, it's Naseema," reported Shahgofta.

Relaxing, he stopped scratching his arm. He was trying to imagine the daughter he had left as a toddler, now shaping flat breads and slapping them to cook inside the open mud tandur. The delicate flesh of her inside upper arms would be scarred from burns caused by the gesture of this slapping motion, as so many girls' arms were, but it would not hinder her methodical contribution to the preparations.

Memories often came knocking on the door to the night manager's mind and transported him back from the store to a moment of his own life at home. He imagined that in a few hours his wife and sisters-in-law would all exchange, moments before breaking the fast, small bowls of what each had cooked. Listening to his wife, Nur Ali was thrown back to childhood again, to that electric moment just before breaking the fast, when he and his brothers had run from house to house carrying platters of whatever his mother had prepared that day, and rushed to make it home with platters from the other homes in time to begin the meal together.

"How about you," Shahgofta asked. "How is your fast going, and what are you eating tonight?"

"When can I possibly break the fast here?" Nur Ali barked back angrily, resuming furious scratching again, and ignoring the unbidden tears that had welled in his eyes. "I can't get a break at dusk, as that's a busy time in the store with a steady flow of customers. Same thing in the morning. They don't fast here, and they don't understand if you want to close the doors and observe rituals. Besides," he added, "I have no appetite for the food here. How can I eat when I worry about you all the time? Sometimes I don't eat for days, and it doesn't have anything to do with the fast. A guy arrived recently from Pakistan and brought an array of sweets from home to share with the guys from Swat. I swear, I couldn't take a single one."

"Why not," asked Shahgofta, not understanding the dilemma.

"I told you, my heart is too heavy. Have you heard from the boys?" he changed topics, repeating himself from earlier. It was easier to talk about others than himself. "How is Sher Banu doing? Do you all have enough food and kerosene for the lamps?" He shifted his weight from one foot to the other and gently rubbed his lower back again to lessen the pain. A flood of unrelated questions spilled from him without pause to reflect the surging anxiety that overflowed in his mind.

Nur Ali had seen both his sons married in his absence. When Ahmad was married to Rabia, the *qaida* had planned and orchestrated every step of the process, but with so much anger and anxiety over not being there in person, he had not kept a good memory of it. It was his brother, Mahmad Ali, who stood in for him at both weddings and who oversaw the choice of Rabia for Ahmad.

16

Sher Banu was Nur Ali's mother's niece turned daughter-in-law four years earlier when she was married to Iqbal, his middle son. It was Shahgofta who informed her husband during one of their nightly conversations that their son was becoming impatient and needed to be married. Although the *qaida* was heavily disappointed, he could not oversee the event in person. He had long ago consulted with Sher Banu's father about eventually obtaining his daughter for Iqbal, and Nur Ali had the comfort of knowing the two youngsters were betrothed before his departure to America. He maintained more control and composure over this wedding.

Nur Ali seized on his wife's momentary silence to recall details of the event.

"You haven't forgotten the day of the proposal, have you? After calling the girl's father myself, from right here in the 7-Eleven, I instructed you to go with gifts of sweets and a suit of clothes for her and her mother, along with your sisters-in-law and, and my brother as my representative, to officially open the engagement."

"How could I forget?" Shahgofta retorted. "I had to report every detail of that visit to you, how our future daughter-in-law was wearing a pink suit with her pant cuffs appropriately loose, not fashionably tight like they wear them in the cities. Her pretty face didn't once crack a smile, and she kept her eyes downcast, signaling respect and modesty toward her prospective in-laws."

Nur Ali smiled with comfort, recalling the warmth of that moment. Reliving positive situations from the past with his wife brought him consolation and hope, momentarily uplifting his spirit.

"And," added Shahgofta, still recalling the conversation from the past regarding Sher Banu, "I had to report to you that she had herself prepared delicious tea—heavy with milk and sugar—and tasty samosas for the visit, showing not only that she could cook but that she would honor guests. You didn't let a single detail unaccounted for. And then that the girl, in her embarrassment, had to whisper her consent to the proposal in her mother's ear, not wanting to appear too forward. How could I forget all of that? We must have talked well over two hours that day!"

"Yes," agreed Nur Ali, now laughing, relaxed. The itching had stopped. "And then our son thanked me for arranging the engagement and marriage, and I counseled him, as I had his older brother earlier, to look after his wife and have many children with her. I recall my exact words to him: 'Remember to let her go home occasionally to visit and assist her own mother; that way she'll be content and take good care of Bibi.' I knew that Sher Banu would now join our first daughter-in-law Rabia to relieve you of your workload. See, I know how to keep you taken care of."

"Hmph," sounded Shahgofta's voice in the receiver.

"Once they were married, I had to maintain control over the realignment of family relations. Remember the day Sher Banu's sister came to visit the new bride and happened to be there when I made my daily phone call? I asked her, 'So, did you come to see your sister or my daughter-in-law?' She stammered before answering, 'Your daughter-in-law, *Qaidada.*'"

Nur Ali insisted on being called the *qaida*, *Qaidada*, and he took his role seriously. When his grandchildren addressed him on the phone as "Baba" or "Abu"—the typical term of address for a grandfather—he berated their parents, reminding them to teach the children to call him *Qaidada*. His own children called him this to emphasize his leadership role. Pashtuns rarely, if ever, used official names when addressing each other. Addressing someone by their proper name showed a lack of respect on the same level as looking someone square in the eye, so Pashtuns had a sophisticated system of naming by using nicknames and kinship terms of endearment—Brother, Sister, Boy, Auntie, or Uncle—to address each other and avoid using proper names. As a result of this deference, there were older women whose names had simply been forgotten from lack of use.

The political climate in Swat had resulted in many Pashtuns being up-rooted from their homes and villages, exiled and thrown into social mélanges of strangers for work and survival, and they often didn't even know each other's names. Even half a world away from home, however, the culture of respect for their elders dominated. Other 7-Eleven employees, for the most part from the same culture, and younger than Nur Ali addressed him as "Kaka" (paternal uncle), "Mama" (maternal uncle), or "Lala" (older brother), each of these displaying respect toward an elder.

The *qaida* suspected that sometime after their wedding and the birth of their first child, Iqbal had begun neglecting Sher Banu, who was now again pregnant, and so Nur Ali took it on himself to look after her with special care. He recalled a woman from his childhood, suffering from grief induced madness over the absence of her husband who was working in the Gulf, and he would do anything to prevent this sense of abandonment in his own household, even as the girl's father-in-law.

"Does she have everything she needs?" Nur Ali asked Shahgofta now about his daughter-in-law. "Put her on the phone. I burn with anxiety over you guys." Never having actually lived with Sher Banu under his roof, the proud father only heard her respectful voice each time she spoke with him, and it filled him with a sense of peace. It resonated with order and equanimity.

"Salam alaykum, *Qaidada*."

"Walaykum salam, child. How are you?" He listened intently for what he might hear in her voice behind the words.

"Well, *Qaidada*. How are you doing?" Her voice was gentle, caressing, content for now.

"How is your baby? Do you need anything for her?"

"No, thank you, *Qaidada*. She is walking now, eating well, and getting fat."

"Are you eating well? Do you have meat? Do you have everything you need?" He felt the knot well up in his stomach the way it did when he craved to perform his family duty but felt alienated by time and space. Without thinking, he relieved the intense itch on his arm, rubbing his sleeve over it with force.

"Of course, *Qaidada*. We're not lacking anything." Sher Banu never asked her father-in-law for anything.

"You make sure and take some of the money I send for yourself and the children. Don't let anyone say that I don't provide for my family, you hear?" He was scratching furiously.

"Yes, *Qaidada*. You're very kind, and you look after us well."

"Now put Bibi back on." This name was used to address both mothers and matriarchs.

Tonight's conversation had lasted over an hour, and Shahgofta asked, "Is that it?"

"Why, are you in a rush? Have you done your noon prayers? I'll send money in a few days. You make sure everyone gets a fair share. Give some extra to Sher Banu and Rabia so they can get things for their kids."

"I always see to them as you ask. Our own children, as well as both our daughters-in-law and their children, have all they need. As do your sisters-in-law Sabina, Salma and Lawangina and their children. You look after everyone."

As clan elder, Nur Ali had say and authority over his brothers and sisters-in-law. He was responsible for them and everyone in the family compound, which legitimately belonged to him by both family and Muslim laws of inheritance.

"And start to get new clothes ready for Eid," pushed on the *qaida*, referring to the post-Ramadan holiday. "Everyone needs new clothes. We may be poor, but we have what we need: food, shelter, family, and enough for new clothes and charitable donations at Eid. Allah says we should not be greedy for more." As head of the clan, it was important for Nur Ali to remind them that he provided amply for his family, that they all had what they needed, and could perform their religious rites. At the same time, he often preached against greed and excess to his family, as his father had to him.

As with most nights when time allowed, Nur Ali called home twice that night, and was met with a different atmosphere just a few hours later. The hours in-between had gone on as usual for the night manager. He had entertained a long chat with his friend, Bacha Gol, who regularly purchased prepaid phone cards for Nur Ali and had them delivered to him by Mir Zaman, a mutual friend and cab driver, during his shift. Bacha Gul called each night to ask if a card was needed.

"Salam alaykum," began the *qaida*, unaware of who had picked up the phone.

"Walaykum salam, *Qaidada,*" replied his brother's wife, Sabina, in an agitated voice that announced trouble and made Nur Ali stand upright.

Shahgofta lived in the same compound with her three sisters-in-law and two daughters-in-law, and Nur Ali exchanged greetings with each of the women as often as he could, asking each in turn about her children and about the general situation. While his sister, Naheela, had married and moved to another compound, his brothers had brought their wives to the parental compound.

Sabina and Lawangina passed the receiver between them to report to their brother-in-law that a bus traveling through Mingora had been burned down just hours hour before, and three young men had been shot right in the middle of the bazaar. They also repeated the report regarding the boys being harassed and interrogated about the adult males in their homes on their way back from school.

"My God! Was it the Bearded Ones?" Nur Ali questioned his sisters-in-law about the shooting, using a term Swatis had coined to refer to the Taliban.

"No," replied Sabina. "It was the soldiers."

"Was there anyone from our village? Anyone we know?" Nur Ali was desperate for more details and grasped for news as he did every day.

"One of those killed was the grandson of the old midwife widow from the next village."

"Oh my God! Those dogs! The bastards! Are there no more Muslims left in our country?" cried out Nur Ali, reiterating his earlier outrage. "God will eventually wipe them out the way they are wiping out the Pashtuns."

Nur Ali's phone card had signaled a minute remaining when Shahgofta got back on the phone. "Talk to me," he told her. "No, wait, I have a customer."

"What do you want me to tell you?" asked Shahgofta.

"Anything. Just talk to me so I can hear your voice. Talk till the minutes run out." She kept him anchored in the present. He knew that the moment they stopped talking, he would be left to his reminiscences.

PAKISTAN BEFORE

"Wake up. Come eat breakfast before daylight." It was the voice of Nur Ali's mother, Bibi, calling him urgently from across the room where she sat on a low stool over a small fire, gently slapping the bread dough between her palms and onto the griddle to fry. Her long thin face and pronounced nose flickered with the flames against the shadow of her veil. The kerosene lamp was already lit in a far corner of the courtyard. The smell of smoke, oil, and frying dough announced the special crispy treat. It was the first year that Nur Ali would attempt the entire fast along with the adults during Ramadan, known in Swat as Rozha. Until now, his tenth year, they had been lenient with him about the fast, allowing him to sneak in bread and water when needed to stave off the hunger pangs, especially during the long summer days. It was different with his sister, who had been obliged to begin fasting like an adult at a younger age. Fasting now was a matter of competition, to see who could emerge with an intact thirty-day record without having broken the fast due to illness or travel. Right now, Nur Ali knew he must eat the meal his mother had prepared because it would have to last him throughout the day, from sunrise until the village preacher, the mullah, made the official call at dusk, when everyone could once again eat.

Although this special pre-dawn meal was eaten in silence in the dark by the heat of his mother's fire, barely a greeting or conversation with anyone during this month could go without the standard questions around the fast.

"Are you fasting? What did you eat last night? What are you eating tonight? Have you broken any days?"

Nur Ali had teased his younger sister, Naheela, when she was obliged to fast at age eight, and now it was her turn to challenge him and see if he could make it. "What's the matter? Can't you keep up with me?" she taunted her brother. "Is your stomach on fire yet? You started out on easy street, and now it's your turn!"

Not only was fasting during Rozha a competition and a matter of honor, it was a shared community experience. Everyone went through it together. Any day Nur Ali broke his fast would have to be made up later in the year, something made more difficult by the fact that he would endure it in isolation, surrounded by food and other people eating. He had grown up hearing that for his people, the Pashtuns of Swat, unlike for other Muslims, the Rozha fast was performed flawlessly, and lack of compliance was not tolerated. He had listened to his aunts and other female relatives bickering and teasing each other about their failure to keep the fast when they had their periods. During the first few days, his stomach groaned with the pain of retraction, making it almost impossible to focus on any task. He and his family waited patiently for the village mullah to sound the evening hour, time to eat a morsel and then a full meal, in which he always claimed he could taste the hunger and desire it had been prepared with.

By the middle of the month, his stomach grew accustomed to the repeated starve-and-stuff process, and it slowly began to contract so that even the voraciousness at the evening meal decreased, if not the passion. Despite adjusting to the physical discomfort, people weakened and slowed toward the latter part of the month. The abdominal burn was constant.

Nur Ali's father often read from the Quran to the family, or re-preached the mullah's Friday sermon at home for the benefit of the women who could not go to the mosque. He also used the time of abstention to remind the household why they were fasting. Nur Ali soaked in every word his father repeated each year during Rozha.

"The last few days are the most trying for all of us," his father proclaimed. "By the end of the day, people are weak and angry in the last hours before they can eat. This is when Allah is testing us, testing our patience, our ability to resist desire. This is when we must prove we are stronger than others. This is also why it's important for us to eat the special foods that your mother prepares: the warm cream and butter drunk before sunrise, along with lentils and rice, and the fried bread are all calculated to give you the nutrients you need to get through the day and perform your tasks. These foods are prescribed by Allah with care and precision." He spoke, stroking his beard, while everyone worked busily but wordlessly around him. And he would read passages from the Quran to help pass the time. But the most important lesson he taught his children about Ramadan and fasting was that everything in Islam was geared to teach an understanding of human misery and suffering, of living life with humility. What his father failed to tell them, that Nur Ali discovered only later, was that some adults secretly took valium to help them get through the fast.

"Rozha is there for us to learn the hunger of the poor," his father would emphasize, "and to then be more sympathetic toward them. The pain we suffer in our stomachs is to teach us the dull pain that the ill live with. As long as you have not suffered this hunger and pain, you will never understand mankind, and you will walk through life proud and untouched, never going anywhere." The lessons he learned from his father during Ramadan were instilled in Ali Nur for life.

On this first morning of the fast, Nur Ali and his three brothers had consumed their pre-dawn fried bread with the rice and lentils for protein and energy to last through the day, and had drunk the warm milk combined with cream and butter that their mother had prepared in large quantity for the family. Bellies filled, they watched her extinguish the fires for the day, and call their sister, Naheela, who dutifully hiked up her sleeves, adjusted her veil around her head and shoulders, and gathered up the dishes. A long black braid hung down her back, thickened by the yarn one woven in with it as she set about washing and cleaning, scrubbing the blackened pots with handfuls of straw.

Nur Ali and his three brothers headed to the orchards to pick apples, pears, apricots, and walnuts destined for the market that day. These had to be picked, sorted, and brought in large baskets to their father's shop in the bazaar before the boys headed down the road to school. On any morning outside of Rozha, the freshly picked fruit would constitute their breakfast, but this first time of picking and abstaining, of full participation in the fast of Rozha, marked Nur Ali's transition into adulthood. The subtle conscious resistance to biting into the juicy plump orange apricots or fragrant pears reminded him of his mission and made him puff with pride.

Nur Ali, being the oldest of the four brothers, held Yusuf Ali's hand, while Mahmad Ali walked tiredly behind them not quite awake yet as the sun rose over the mountains. The boys respected their older brother, and now they also admired his ability to fast alongside the adults.

Sardar Ali, still too young for school, spent his days at home with his mother, sometimes running to the shop with his father or down to the men's washing area of the river. This was a favorite activity for the boys, and Nur Ali met his brothers and friends there on summer days. As children, the four brothers spent most of their time together, either at home, in the village, or at school, but play time by the water was an exceptional treat. In the sun, men and boys would wash and dry their pants on the stones and swim with their shirts wrapped around their waists. Older men would sit on their heels contemplating the angry gray river, rinsing their feet, hands, and faces to prepare for prayers, or they would lay their blankets and a stone down to create a makeshift prayer mat. Boys' squeals and cries would echo above the sound of the rushing water over the rocks as they played in the sun. And on either side of the river rose the sullen green mountains, tiered with terraces for crops.

As for Naheela, she worked at home with her mother, and followed the narrow dirt path with the other neighboring girls to the nearest water pump twice a day to fill the round metal pots with water for the household. Because Nur Ali's family house was somewhat removed and higher up the mountain from the village center, a single pump serviced it and the two other compounds along the path that climbed from the village. Naheela could look down the lush green mountainside to the flat mud rooftops of the village houses, each with its opening and ladder leading down to its courtyard. No individual home had running water, and the three public faucets positioned throughout their village of Khwaza Khel only came on at two specific times each day, providing an occasion for young girls to gather and gossip. Their stories and critiques mimicked those of their mothers, which they had heard previously in their home courtyard. Nur Ali was soon to discover that for him the best part of Rozha, this first time and all subsequent years, was the bustling activity surrounding the break of the fast as evening drew near, followed by the relaxed atmosphere of each evening once everyone's hunger had once again been sated.

Prior to eating, Nur Ali accompanied the men, who came and went, bringing large heavy tins of water to fill the round metal pots in the courtyard, supplementing what the girls brought in during the day. They balanced two heavy tins at each end of a bar across their shoulders and slowly and laboriously made their way from the village up the path to the family compound. His mother, aunts, cousins, and sister each were occupied at a task to prepare the evening meal. They chopped onions and tomatoes, and ground garlic, coriander, and peppers for garnish. They pounded fresh meat on a flat stone with a smaller rock to add to the stew. Green peppers or eggplant were added in later, as were more tomatoes. The air began to saturate with the mouth-watering fragrance of spices and cooking smells. Several small fires burned at once in the courtyard for various dishes, and the flames in the tandur died, leaving coals and scalding walls against which the girls threw the flat breads. One scooped handfuls of dough from the basket, shaped them into balls and set these on a flour-covered flat basket, while another flattened them, slapping each ball from hand to hand until it was ten to twelve inches in diameter. It was the same gesture Nur Ali had so often seen the women prepare dung cakes, which they smacked against the sunny wall of the house to dry for fuel to be used when there was no wood. After a few minutes, the flat bread was baked, its edges beginning to peel away from the coal heated oven walls and ready to scrape off the oven's inner sides. His mother would sprinkle a few drops of water on it and lay the bread face down on the coals for a few seconds to form a crust. Twenty loaves were required at each meal to feed his entire family.

While the women were busy working, the girls not involved with the bread tended to the babies, carrying them from one spot to the next on their hip, wiping snotty noses and drools with their veil ends or shirt tails. If a baby cried from hunger, the child would lay it in its mother's lap, and mom would let the baby suck on her breast while she continued to labor over the meal. Other girls swept up the food scraps and peels which were discarded onto the mud floor and kept aside for feeding the chickens. And when the multiple dishes were ready, each woman who had been working on a different dish or part of the meal, divided it up into bowls with various destinations throughout the village. Nur Ali and his brothers hustled to deliver these.

The silent agitation of these men and children who transported water and food and moved throughout the village at a rapid pace is precisely what remained rooted in Nur Ali's mind now so far away in a convenience store in America where none of this existed, where life moved at a different cadence . The thought of these moments brought him solace when he found himself alienated from them. He could see them, excited and driven by adrenaline, on a mission to deliver each container and bread to its proper location, and bring one home in exchange, in time to sit for dinner.

It was imperative that everyone have food ready to break the fast just as the mullah wailed out the time over the village speaker: the religious students living at the mosque, the sick in the clinic, and certain designated beggars, all had to be fed. Then there were bowls exchanged for different bowls from relatives' households, so that in the end, Nur Ali and his family sat down to a lavish meal with a wide variety of hot and cold dishes. Sometimes, if they were caught still en route when the mullah's call sounded, they would quickly dip into one of the dishes for a bite to satisfy tradition. Nur Ali's mother made sure the boys carried dates in their pockets for this purpose. Dinners during Rozha were better than any other dinners during the year.

After dinner, the men would leave for the mosque to pray, socialize, and smoke while the women remained to clean up and scrub the pots blackened from the fire with bits of straw. With bellies full and darkness upon them, everyone moved more slowly. Yelling ceased, and a hush fell on the valley. There were no street lights in Khwaza Khel. Inside, homes were lit with a single bare bulb, but these went out frequently with the brown-outs that ran through the valley, and dim kerosene lamps provided the default lighting. Daylight permitted activity, and darkness brought on calm. If the men had to be out after dark, they carried flashlights. Time was measured not by clocks but by the calls to prayer, based on the sun's position, so that days were truly longer or shorter depending on the season. Only after all was cleaned up over quiet chatter and the dough was prepared for the pre-dawn meal did the women take turns to perform their prayers on the straw mat reserved for home devotions.

As a boy, Nur Ali had escorted his mother and aunts and cousins through-out the mountains and into the village for structured outings. Forbidden from circulating in public on their own, women often used young male children to escort them. They went daily to certain houses in Khwaza Khel for Quranic recitation, which he was not invited to attend after he had reached a certain age. Large groups of girls and women sat cross-legged around a room, each with folded pages propped on a criss-crossed wood panel in front of them. Rocking and swaying, they memorized and recited the holy texts in Arabic. The written texts served as a memory prompt, as the women, being Pashto speakers, were incapable of reading Arabic.

He also escorted his mother for visits of inquiry after this or that person's health, or at weddings, boys' births, circumcisions, or funerals. Participation at these visits was important for her, and he vicariously took in her involvement while playing with the other boys or sitting on a nearby cot observing her and listening to the gossip.

One such time that remained engraved in Nur Ali's memory was when his mother had him escort her on a house visit to ask about a young woman whose husband had left to work in the Gulf. Despite the winter rain and mud-filled paths, they had trekked down the mountain to Khwaza Khel and sloshed through the muddy alleys to the woman's house, where other women were already gathered to cry alongside and console the young wife. His mother had asked Nur Ali to remain, not knowing how long she would stay. As soon as they entered, a young girl brought them both tea and cakes and set to massaging his mother's, Bibi's, thighs in recognition of the effort it had taken to come visit.

The young wife's mother-in-law, upon prompting, related to Bibi the story while Nur Ali sat all ears, taking it in.

"He came for a short leave, but had to go back to work, and she is overwhelmed with grief. She just sits and weeps all day. We all decided that the girl is possessed by jinns, fits of depression, so I went to the mullah to buy a talisman for the girl to ward them off. It cost me eighty rupees."

The mention of jinn, spirits that can help or harm human affairs, made him lean forward. As the oldest brother, Nur Ali had been given a talisman to wear on a string around his neck to ward off evil. He was struck by the harm a man could cause by neglecting his wife. He mused at the resulting depression named "jinn," and wondered about the effectiveness of talismans against them. The memory of this event often haunted him now, as he thought of his own daughter-in-law, Sher Banu, neglected by her husband, his son. Nur Ali had made her his responsibility.

"I'll tell you who needs a talisman against evil spirits," chimed in Bibi. "You know Wazifa's son, the one who is a heroin addict? Well, he's never home, obviously too ashamed in his condition to appear under his parents' roof. His wife, however, in her loneliness, has been seen talking with other men. Such a shame! She's brought dishonor on the family, and there's talk of a public stoning."

So, thought Nur Ali, *she has no recourse for her neglect than to be patient and wear talismans!*

"What a slut!" exclaimed the woman. "The prostitute! She deserves whatever she gets. A woman owes loyalty to her husband and his family. It doesn't matter what he does."

Bibi and the woman continued to visit and gossip while Nur Ali sat quietly on a low stool waiting for his mother, half listening and watching the rainwater fill a canal at the far end of the courtyard in which children washed themselves, their clothes, dishes, and vegetables. But from his unobtrusive position, he unquestioningly absorbed the values of marriage that he took with him into adulthood. He came to understand the position men and women held and that a woman could go mad as a result of her husband's absence.

Nur Ali held closely the precious memories of the few times he had ever spent alone with his father. Of course there were times they worked together in the shop or on a home chore, and of course they prayed together at the mosque, but there were those few times when father and son disappeared alone to enjoy a breezy moment on the rooftop shaded by fruit and nut trees, nibbling on pears and walnuts. These were moments in which the father taught his son life's most valuable lessons.

One his father's favorite topics to preach to the family was hypocrisy. He riled lengthily against the practice, accusing Muslims of acting in non-Muslim ways, among the worst of human crimes in his eyes.

One day, when Nur Ali was engaged with his father on the rooftop for one of their talks, he asked him more about the subject. Wrapped in his brown blanket, knees drawn up to his chest as he sat on his heels, the elder's blackened, sunken eyes squinted as he talked, and the boy eagerly soaked in every word coming from his father's red-hennaed beard, only to hear them exit his own lips as he aged. "Hypocrites," explained father to son, "claim to be Muslim while they either commit non-compliant sins, exhibit pride, or misconstrue verses from the Quran."

"But why would they do that?" asked the child. "To justify violent or abusive behavior," replied the pious father. "Such people are the vilest of the vile on earth."

"I'll try to stay away from hypocrites, then, and not to become one, myself," solemnly promised the boy.

"And you must learn to recognize the Kafirs," added Nur Ali's father as a warning to his son, "those who worship stones, objects, pictures, and idols. Stay away from them. They are not like us. We follow only our holy Quran."

"Father," Nur Ali continued to question his elder, "tell me about Issa Massi." This was the Christian Christ that he had heard the mullah talk about in a sermon.

"He will come back as a Muslim," explained his father, "and the whole world will unite as Muslims." He taught his son that Christianity was weakening and that the holy jihad would eventually take over the world.

Stopping only to spit the juices from the tobacco he had balled up between his lower lip and teeth, Nur Ali's father spoke about the people in the sky who have no body or physical senses, but only souls. "But we," he added, "are the most complete people because we have not only minds and hearts, we also have bodies that need to eat, feel, and make love."

And from his limited knowledge of the world beyond his small region of Khwaza Khel, Nur Ali's father taught his son about the various lands and animals that God had created on the earth. "There is a desert, where the land is not green like ours, where there is no monsoon like we have, but the earth is dry and soft so that your foot sinks into it with every step. And in the desert is an animal called the camel with feet so large and soft he can easily walk in it. He needs very little to eat or drink to survive, and people call him the 'airplane of the desert.'"

With these outlooks, rhythms, and experiences, Nur Ali grew up a relatively happy boy in the isolated Swat valley, protected by the lush mountains, the river, and the movement of everyday life and repeated seasons. Life was simple and certain. He savored these memories, which represented a time of order, when things made sense . He had watched his father, the clan elder, rule over the family decisions and honor, and dictate who could go where for what reason, and he knew, growing up, that this would one day be his own mission. Little could he imagine, or be prepared for the fact that he would do so from far away, from the chaotic world beyond Swat where few knew or understood the life of this idyllic place.

7-ELEVEN

Some forty-five years later, Nur Ali found himself in an American inner city 7-Eleven, where he had been continuously managing the night shift for over thirteen years. He was a small man, like most Pashtuns from the mountains of Pakistan's northern Swat Valley, with a slight build and a smiling, gentle appearance and quiet step that welcomed customers. Soft spoken and mild mannered, he always had a kind word for neighborhood Muslim children he recognized, who came with their parents to buy candy from the store's prized candy selection and display, or fill cups from the slushy machine. "Children," had preached his father, "are innocent, weak, and vulnerable; they deserve to be treated with sympathy and gentleness."

"Have you been behaving for your parents?" Nur Ali would ask them. "Don't forget to bring something for your older sister," he added if he knew there was a cloistered female sibling at home. "And do as your mother tells you," he admonished with a smile.

The aging 7-Eleven employee was fair-skinned and wore his thick gray hair straight down over his forehead. He wore a long, straggly beard, which completed his foreign appearance. His worn khakis were loose-fitting, as was the button-down shirt, often stained and dirty, but he didn't pay it any attention. He changed his clothes twice a week, as he had done all his life, and saw no need to alter this. He walked lightly on his feet, barely audible to others, with intentional movements and never a shuffle. He scratched his arms continually, but didn't know or care if the itching was from a rash or bug bites. It was just always there. Sometimes it was so bad he crossed them and scratched both arms from the side, looking like he was cold. He was polite with customers but spoke a bare minimum, in a heavily accented broken English. He spoke no more than needed to exist and perform his job until he returned home.

Nur Ali, who had become a grandfather during his fifteen year absence from Khwaza Khel, worked his night shift mostly alone. A co-worker, Michael, stayed until ten o'clock or midnight, and then Nur Ali remained alone until Layla came to take over at seven. Younger co-workers, respectful of his advanced age, saw to it that he did not have to perform any heavy tasks like shovel snow, mop floors, or carry out the trash. He mostly tended the counter and took care of the cooler, coffee, and slushy machines. After so many years in the store, he could single-handedly manage the lottery tickets, food orders, money orders, and food stamps, just about anything to do with running the store, all while holding a conversation on the phone. His reliability and consistent loyalty represented a tremendous asset to the franchisees, who had a fast turnover rate of night shift workers. They trusted him implicitly, made him night manager, and tasked him with training new employees.

Nur Ali's friend, Bacha Gul, also from Swat, who worked the night shift at another 7-Eleven across town, called him in the hollow hours of each night, so they could keep each other company. Mostly they gossiped about people and events in their exiled Swat community, resolved phone card issues, shared complaints of aches and pains, and advised each other on store details. If one or the other had to deal with a customer, they knew to wait patiently before resuming the conversation. Bacha Gul provided Nur Ali with phone cards, and although the two rarely saw each other, they used another mutual acquaintance from Swat, Mir Zaman, to shuttle the cards and payment with his taxi. This proved to be a near nightly experience. Mir Zaman also occasionally went to New York, the only place Nur Ali knew he could get *naswar*, the tobacco-snuff he and so many other Swati men were addicted to. He would roll it into a ball and suck on it the same way he had watched his father and other men in Khwaza Khel do. The younger generation favored cigarettes to *naswar*. Nur Ali's calls to Mir Zaman grew more desperate when his supply was running low. *Naswar* sold for three hundred dollars per kilo, a quantity far beyond his need, so when he could get some, he called other Swati friends and acquaintances he knew used it to try and share the order.

How had he come here? Nur Ali and his father and three brothers had long ago decided how they would divide their efforts to best look after the family.

"Nur Ali and Yusuf Ali will go abroad to earn an income and send money home," had dictated their father . "Mahmad Ali and Sardar Ali will remain home to look after the household and the women."

"I'll go to Qatar for work," had announced Yusuf Ali, who had friends already there.

Indirectly, Nur Ali had found his way to America where, now, the only member of his family, he had nothing invested in his existence. Like so many immigrants on the same mission, his sole purpose was to earn and send money home to his immediate as well as extended family, and eventually return home to retire. It was a seemingly reliable plan, popularly lived and applauded among his compatriots, of whom only a few brought over their families and intended to assimilate and remain. The plan guaranteed a good return on investment, but required years of social isolation. He knew from the start what he was getting into. Many families in Swat had at least one male member working in the Gulf or elsewhere for income.

Loyal to his mission, Nur Ali never bought any food from the store, and never lost his focus on saving money to send home. His objective was clear and had been established and maintained intact since he had come to America: For fifteen years, he had worked steadily and sent money home to his village on a regular basis through his brother, Mahmad Ali, at first, and later through a cousin, Na'im. The money was to support the family, as well as to save for his retirement. In addition, he had lent money to various friends and relatives over the time for exceptional projects they needed, expecting to recuperate this on his return. He calculated where the money went and how his personal savings were growing. He was satisfied that over the fifteen years of working in America, he had put away a substantial sum to meet his needs, and knew with whom each bit was stashed. No difficulty he encountered in his daily life in exile mattered, as long as the goal was being met. Devoted to his mission, he even kept a cup of water he drew from the restroom faucet rather than pay for bottled water. He had sent home over three hundred thousand dollars, or forty million rupees, and evaluated his net worth to be adequate. Though he inhabited and worked in America, he lived his life in Khwaza Khel.

Although Nur Ali may at one point have considered bringing his sons here to work, he had never thought of bringing his family to settle here. There was no question of assimilation on any level in his mind. As such, he had no reason to learn English, and sought no social ties with any Americans. Over the years, he had always rented a room in a cheap apartment with other Pashtuns, or at least Pakistanis. Currently, he resided with two Baluchis and a Punjabi, although they barely spent time together.

The community of Pashtuns from Swat exiled in the same city was very connected, and extended to include all Pashto speakers, Afghan or Pakistani . They all knew each other, shared housing, networked to find each other jobs, worked together, shared news from their home villages, and looked after each other in times of sickness or disaster. They worked several markets throughout the city: 7-Elevens, fried chicken take-outs, gas stations, auto shops, and food carts, not to mention taxi services.

The Pashtun community, like most immigrant communities, drew from each other for services and advice, for language reasons as well as trust. They exchanged goods and services among themselves; they dealt strictly in cash, and they remained highly distrustful of American authorities and other ethnic groups. They borrowed from each other and sought medical advice among their own. Pockets of labor, especially where franchises were concerned, were run by families or fellow compatriots. Dunkin Donuts, for instance, was held by other South Asian groups, as were many gas stations, motels, and auto repair centers.

As with other ethnic minority groups, there were illegals among them, and even those who were legal lived in fear of exposure and deportation if they came into contact with authorities of any kind. Those seeking asylum or citizenship for themselves and their families also kept a low profile, dealt with issues from within the community, and refrained from reaching out to social or legal services. Since 2001 and the events of 9/11, the immigrant community, especially Pakistanis, had become a target of hatred and mistrust, and had turned even more fervently in on itself, relying on one another. Discussions at the mosque were dominated by stories of having experienced assaults, and warnings to keep a low profile.

Nur Ali had fallen in with the 7-Eleven group, and was perfectly content there, convinced it was the best job for him. Each time a young man arrived from Swat and called him for help, Nur Ali described his job to him. "7-Eleven is one of the greatest opportunities in America. There are thousands of stores in this city alone. And the bosses here, they're Muslim, Afghan, and they treat you well. They'll pay you cash and start you out at six dollars and fifty cents an hour, but if you stay, they'll take you up to seven dollars fast. They're good people."

Each night after one o'clock, already on his feet for six hours , Nur Ali wiped off the counter for himself, as if preparing the space for ritual. After glancing around to make sure there was no one, and everything was in order, he looked for a moment at the store phone which sat beside the cash register, hidden to customers behind a sign that read "No change for $100 bills." He deliberately picked up the receiver, allowed himself to sit on the stool he kept behind the counter for momentary rests between tending to customers or to store tasks, and punched the numbers to his first call. On the counter beside him lay the calling card containing the allotted number of minutes he had purchased.

For the next few hours of his shift until the early morning rush, holding that receiver, the night manager of the 7-Eleven returned vicariously to Khwaza Khel and the family compound, where he re-assumed his role as clan leader. He talked non-stop in a loud, abrasive, gravelly voice to family back home, or with other exiled Pashtuns in town. The grit in his tone on the phone was markedly different from that of his store employee tone. Occasionally, when he dealt with store customers, he switched suddenly back to his gentle voice to insert into these conversations the few terse stock phrases of politeness he knew in English. It was the same thing his colleagues all did in their respective convenience stores, fast food eateries and food carts, taxis or gas stations; they were all accustomed to the momentary suspension of another world's dialogue to allow words of service to a customer.

PAKISTAN BEFORE

Nur Ali's wedding day was a memory he often dwelt on, savoring every minute of the dream. Whether wrapped in his blanket on his bed in the apartment or standing behind the 7-Eleven counter in quiet moments of night, it brought him solace, a connection to a world he partially idealized and partially knew was no longer his.

Being the eldest, Nur Ali was the first of his siblings to get married. At eighteen, he had finished school and was working the family lands as well as helping his father in the store. It was around this time that he came home one day after closing the shop to find both his parents wishing to speak with him.

"It's time you were married and brought in a wife," his father abruptly announced.

"We think your cousin, Shahgofta, is the best match," added his mother.

Nur Ali said nothing, but nodded his consent. This was the cousin with whom he had grown up in the same compound. She had played alongside him and his sister, brothers, and other cousins. As a boy he had on occasion scurried through the bazar with Naheela and Shahgofta running errands for their mothers before the girls reached the age to remain home. They had spent hours with other children playing the popular stone game.

Sitting on their heels in a circle, they would take turns tossing a stone while picking up an increasing number of stones from the ground before catching the falling stone, all with one hand. Shahgofta was quick-handed and somehow managed to beat the boys. They had wandered through the fruit orchards picking pears and walnuts to bring home, and had harvested corn and picked tomatoes from the family plots.

That night, his father and uncle formally visited Shahgofta's father with some gifts and asked him to give them Shahgofta for Nur Ali. When they returned with a positive reply, there was dancing and celebration in the compound.

"Finally," cried Naheela with delight. "I'm going to have a sister to share the housework with."

"And I'll have someone to take over some of my burden," sighed Bibi, Nur Ali's mother.

"The best part," added Mahmad Ali, "is that we don't have to worry about keeping them apart during the engagement period while living in the same compound."

Shahgofta's family had already moved away from the compound, as her father, Nur Ali's uncle, had separated from the family and established himself independently in the village. He owned two buffalos and a dairy shop in Khwaza Khel where he sold fresh milk and yogurt.

"Your brother and his wife," announced his father to the boys, "will take over your uncle's former room in the compound, so the girls who have been sleeping there will have to go elsewhere." Unless there was a spare room for them, older children had to remain in their parents' room until they were married.

The very next day, Nur Ali's sisters and cousins, with his mother and aunts, set about purchasing and preparing gifts to offer Shahgofta's family at the formal henna and sweets party, which would seal the engagement. They worked long hours to produce a collection of ornate hair braids with tassels and gold and silver threads, sending the young children several times a day to the shop to get materials. They purchased bangles and cloth from salesmen who wandered through the village lanes hawking their wares with repeated calls meant to waft into courtyards filled with female clientele. "Beautiful bangles of every size!" They called from the street. "Fabrics for every occasion!"

When Bibi, Nur Ali's mother, heard them coming, she grabbed her large veil from the hook where it hung, and ran to the compound entrance. Remaining hidden, she hissed at the vendors to beckon them to her door, at the same time signaling her daughters and nieces to retreat to their rooms out of sight. Her sisters-in-law, being older, could assist her with the purchase, as well as they could act as witnesses that Bibi would not create a scandal by interacting alone with a strange man inside the family walls.

Although they spoke Pashto, these vendors were not ethnic Pashtun, but Punjabis, held in lower esteem by Pashtuns. As a result of their lower status, it was understood that they could enter homes strictly for purposes of conducting sales, as long as they exercised proper etiquette. Fabric, jewelry, shoes, household items, and fruit were sold in this manner, marketed to women at home whose presence would not normally be tolerated in public markets.

" Ah, for your first son's wedding," beamed the salesman careful to keep his eyes on his wares, "Bibi, I can get you the best fabrics from Peshawar and Rawalpindi in the most fashionable colors ."

"Just get eight yards of fabric per suit," her sisters had warned her in advance. "Three for a long-sleeved dress and five for the full baggy trousers. And no need to sew them. Just offer them the eight yards to make a suit to their liking. The fashion changes all the time."

"You know, with the reduced bunch at the waist, you can get a suit made with just five yards," suggested the salesman.

"We don't do that here. We use a full eight yards, and do no reduction at the waist. The extra yardage is our tradition here, and it adds warmth in the winter."

Bibi's cousins commended her choices, but added, "Some of us prefer our dresses longer or shorter, or the trouser cuff looser or tighter over the ankle. Some folks like a loose open sleeve, while others may want it to snap tight around the wrist. By the time these women get to making a suit from the cloth, they may have changed their habits."

As it was, Bibi needed enough for individual suits for each woman in Shahgofta's family, as well as some extras for other relatives. And her own son needed a new suit. The salesman, unprepared on this first visit, offered to return with better, more suitable cloth the following week. Still, Bibi took sufficient yardage of his nicer fabric for two suits to start.

"I'm so glad I'm not an Afghan," she sighed as the cloth merchant left. Her sisters laughed with understanding. Since the 1980s Afghan refugees had rented houses in Swat to escape the grueling heat of summer in the Peshawar Valley. "They take eight to ten yards just for their trousers!"

This set all the women into peals of laughter. "Those Afghan women can sit on thorn bushes and not feel it!" cried out one, barely able to finish.

"I've heard that in the camps," chimed in Bibi in a hushed voice, "fights erupt regularly at the public wells over dress between rural women, who are determined to continue wearing their heavy clothing, and the city women, who have adapted the lighter Pakistani dress to better tolerate the intense heat of the Peshawar Valley."

"It's cruel and heartless," added her sister. "The old country women shame their younger urban sistersand stand in their way to stop them getting water from the wells."

Six months following much preparation, Nur Ali and Shahgofta were married in full Swati tradition. Nur Ali felt nervous as he woke up that spring morning. The night before, all the women and girls from his compound had paraded down the hillside to the outskirts of the village and through the narrow alleys hugged by mud walls to Shahgofta's house, carrying trays of henna and lit candles for the henna party. Clad in sparking clothes and wearing the jewelry from dowries, they had sung songs to the beat of a tambourine-like drum, and danced in a circle, clapping their hands and turning on themselves.

Despite the bride's excitement, which was of course tinged with nervousness over the wedding, she was expected to exhibit sadness this night, and throughout the evening as she sat with her mother at her side, void of words or facial expression, clad in shiny new clothes and jewels, and covered in veils, her head and eyes remained lowered. Her and her mother's and sisters' tears were symbolic of the looming separation that was about to come between them.

On the eve of her wedding, Shahgofta's female entourage quietly shared the knowledge that Shahgofta no longer belonged to her natal home, but to another, where a new mother and father would now rule over her and determine her destiny. The only spoken interaction between them were hushed commands to each other to fix Shahgofta's veils or to see to the needs of guests.

In contrast to the woe demonstrated by Shahgofta and her female relatives, the women from Nur Ali's house sang and danced in the courtyard and painted the subdued Shahgofta's hand with henna to welcome their new sister, then wrapped her closed fist with a cloth to bind the damp mud-like substance to her skin until the next day. All the women and girls crowded around the trays to grab a fistful of henna to color their own hands and nails.

It was sunny and cool around mid-morning when he and his father, brothers, and cousins marched proudly through the village and mountain paths to Shahgofta's house, accompanied by a drummer and reed flute player. With each step they took, Nur Ali's nervousness grew. He knew his life was about to change forever. The bride, meanwhile, had been prepared and was seated in her tiny caged wedding palanquin with handles, just large enough to hold her sitting cross-legged.

"Is she ready?" bellowed Nur Ali's father, leading the party.

The women sobbed to signal consent.

"Are all her things gathered?" he asked again.

More sighs and moans.   .

The bride embraced her mother, sisters, and other close female relatives and said goodbye to the security and familiarity she had always known. Even though she wasn't going far, it was unknown how soon or how often her husband would allow her to return to her parents' home. They lamented now as she was taken from them.

Piled on top of Shahgofta's caged palanquin were the traditional layers of hand-embroidered silk and brocade sheets and veils, designed to conceal the bride and her tears of separation. Although she knew her cousin, and her mother-in-law was the aunt she had grown up with, Shahgofta was filled with anxiety over what would be expected of her as a wife: no one had spoken to her about what to expect on her wedding night, or about marital relationships. All she knew was that she now belonged to this new family, answerable not only to a husband, but responsible for maintaining his honor by way of her behavior. Love and intimacy were not factored into the marriage equation in this arranged union. Love, everyone had told her, was the result of time and making decisions together, of having come from similar backgrounds so that unexpected differences would not surface over time.

Nur Ali would not actually see his bride until much later. The other men briefly danced around her; then four of them picked up the palanquin, each taking a handle, and lifting it high, began running back up along the narrow mountain path, whooping and singing as the musicians kept their rhythm going. The procession was followed by a drummer and tambourine player. Apart from the bride, the single file of men also carried trunks filled with fabric, jewelry, shoes, tea sets, trays, china plates and kitchen ware, a bedroom set and several low stools—all gifts and part of Shahgofta's dowry, which belonged solely to her.

Arriving at Nur Ali's house, the men deposited the palanquin in the courtyard, and carried the trunks and furniture into the new couple's room. For today, in addition to the guest room reserved for the oldest generation of relatives, neighbors, and village elders, a giant colorful partition had been raised in the middle of the courtyard, so that men and women could maintain gender separation, each on their own side of the courtyard. They could dance, eat and celebrate without reserve, and unrelated villagers and neighbors could attend the party without fear of violating rules of propriety. Of course, as dictated by tradition, only Nur Ali's relatives danced and showed glee. They were adding a member to their work force. Bibi would finally be relieved of some of her duties as her new daughter-in-law took them over. Shahgofta sat motionless, completely covered, eyes downcast, while women took turns to lift her veils and comment on how beautiful she looked. Her own mother and sisters stood by her, also crying, continuously adjusting her veils to spread them out perfectly around her.

The religious ceremony was held in the couple's room off the verandah, presided by the mullah from Khwaza Khel. It was filled with male relatives when Shahgofta, still completely covered and eyes downcast, was escorted inside by Nur Ali's cousin. She was seated next to the groom, whose uncle held a mirror in front of them, in which they each could look at each other, indirectly, symbolically for the first time, although in this case since her father had moved out of the family courtyard a few years ago. It was fitting that Nur Ali, as the oldest brother, would remain to inherit the family home.

The mullah asked the witnesses to testify, and the bride and groom to accept the terms. Just as quickly, Shahgofta was shuffled back out of the room to her spot among the women, and tea was brought in to the men.

Later in the evening, amidst the festivities, Nur Ali came to the women's side of the courtyard and was seated next to his bride for exhibition, without a word. A plate of sweets was held in front of him, and he picked one up and fed it to Shahgofta in silence, while she kept her eyes downcast. The crowd applauded, and this ritual marked the beginning of their married life together.

Now, after so many years, memories of this night brought solace to Nur Ali's exiled existence.

7-ELEVEN

Nur Ali's apartment was a convenient walking distance from the store. He shared a second-floor apartment with three other exiles, Baluchi and Punjabi, with whom he shared little in common other than being Muslim and Pakistani. His room was sparse. There were no photos either framed or on the wall of family or home. They had communicated all these years solely by phone, so there was no occasion to send any photos. Besides, they had never taken any photos, and had none to share. Photographing women was dangerous and could lead to trouble and public viewing. Portrait photos of men were acceptable, but the practice was limited to the wealthy. When it came to his grandchildren—even his adult children he had last seen as toddlers and adolescents—Nur Ali had to imagine their appearance from their voices only and Shahgofta's descriptions.

A narrow single bed occupied one end of the room, while several hooks on the opposite wall held the few clothes he had. He boasted that he held onto a traditional suit of clothes from home that came with him fifteen years ago and that he changed into only when in the privacy of his home to sleep in. Otherwise, he alternated between two pairs of pants and three shirts for work, replacing these at Goodwill when needed. A cardboard box on the floor contained socks, underwear, and his folded pants and shirts. A single pair of sneakers, when not on his feet, lay neatly under the hung clothes.

Nur Ali's brown blanket from Swat lay on his bed, although on cold days he wrapped it around himself in traditional manner, throwing one end up over his shoulder. And sometimes he sat with his knees drawn up wrapped in it simply for comfort, for a momentary escape from his own practicality. It was during these moments, wrapped in the old blanket, holding on to his beard, that he made himself return to memories of his past, of that time of sense and order, where he could regain the calm he needed to apply to the present chaos. He forced himself to see and count the fruit trees in the orchard, to hear the mud squish under his sandals as he climbed the path from Khwaza Khel to the compound, to hear the mullah's call for prayer echo through the valley and up the hills.

He had acquired no other possessions over the years, feeling no need to burden himself with any more than would return home with him. His minimalist approach was born of practicality. Whatever he bought was an intended gift for a family member, such as the much-coveted cell phones. In the corner of his room, tucked behind the clothing box and covered with a towel, sat a second cardboard box, folded shut. It contained items such as cheap plastic toys, women's and children's shoes, jewelry, socks, girls' dresses, and occasionally a cell phone hidden among the clothing and other objects. These were the gifts that Nur Ali kept stocked in his room, and he was in constant pursuit of Pashtuns returning home who could transport small items as gifts for his family who were all he ever thought about.

The roommates shared a kitchen, and although it provided an oven, Nur Ali never used it. He only cooked in an open pot, the way he had seen done by his mother and his wife. No matter what he prepared, apart from rice, he used the same base ingredients, and always kept the kitchen stocked with onions, tomatoes, garlic, oil and spices from the nearby Afghan shop.

Other Pashtun Muslims in town who lived with their family, tended to seek a floorplan which accommodated segregation and allowed direct access to a separate room from the main entrance. This was to receive male guests, who could enter and be entertained without having to cross the kitchen or other areas of the house where women could remain in seclusion. Since Nur Ali lived with three other single men, such a floorplan was not an issue in their apartment. They kept a television in the living room, and shared a Pak-TV plan, which provided news and other programs in Urdu. Nur Ali did not spend many waking hours in his apartment, and his room-mates comprised the least of all his social relationships.

The 7-Eleven, mosque, Western Union shop, and Indian and Afghan food markets were all close by in the ethnic neighborhood where Indians and Pakistanis lived together, and there was hardly any need for Nur Ali to take any public transportation or to venture any farther. He entered the Western Union shop twice a month to send a money order home and felt important in the store's dark air of security behind a layer of steel bars. The chubby Indian with the mustache welcomed him cordially each time from behind his glass window. Occasionally, Nur Ali stopped in the Indian restaurant for some rice and chicken, or just to enjoy a cup of tea and smells of familiar cooking. He felt comfortable in his neighborhood, where children in colorful clothes, women in black full-body veils and in saris were a common sight. There were no banks or a post office nearby, but he had no need for these. And if he ever did need to go anywhere beyond his little world, he could rely on fellow cab drivers.

Apart from his daily visits to the mosque to pray and socialize, the store provided Nur Ali's social life. It was franchised by Momen Khan and his wife, Shiriney, who franchised three other 7-Eleven stores throughout the city and suburbs. Being that Nur Ali worked more hours than anyone at the 7-Eleven, he was especially close with his bosses. Moreover, their hardships struck a similar chord to Nur Ali's, and he felt a common bond with the Afghan couple. When time allowed and the store was quiet, the three of them enjoyed recounting their pasts.

"We fled Kabul as newlyweds in 1984," began Momen Khan on one such occasion, "after the Russians invaded Afghanistan and we moved to the Jalozai refugee camp on the outskirts of Peshawar."

"We were both raised and educated in Kabul added Shiriney, who liked to stress this difference between themselves and other less educated exiles. Momen Khan had attended the Law College at Kabul University, and Shiriney the Medical College, although she had not completed her program.

"Life in the camp was difficult for us," said Momen Khan. "I tried to earn a living in Peshawar, interpreting at a German non-governmental organization, and vying for jobs and resources with the local Pakistani population. But they didn't like us."

Nur Ali interrupted, "I heard the locals in Peshawar resented having to host over two million Afghan refugees while watching them receive items from foreign aid agencies that they couldn't afford for their own homes."

"This is probably true. I heard the same," nodded Momen Khan. "Two of my brothers moved in and out of Afghanistan, participating in the war against the Russians at the time, while my third brother worked in Dubai and sent money home for the family."

"We women also suffered in the camp," chimed in Shiriney. "I was surrounded by other Afghan women with whom I had nothing in common. They mostly came from rural areas, were barely if at all literate, and spoke different languages and dialects. They ate and dressed differently than I did and we bickered over notions of childrearing."

Nur Ali shook his head and clucked his tongue in sign of sympathy. "And you had the heat of Peshawar, too!"

"Don't talk to me about heat," continued Shiriney. "We never had heat and humidity like that in Kabul. Babies' body temperatures soared. The camps offered only fans, and with with all the power cuts, some of us adapted Pakistani dress, using lighter cotton and less yardage. But we were shunned by less educated, rural neighbors. Several times I was denied access to the common water pump on the premise that I was indecently dressed."

"The worst of it," added Sher Alam in support of his wife's description, "is that they threw all Afghan refugees in together with no regard for social, economic, or educational differences between us. We had no choice, since we didn't have the resources to buy a house on our own. We were alienated from the households around us. They resented that we used soap to wash our hands, that we changed our clothes regularly, and bathed every two to three days, that we kept our children clean and well dressed, and that we took them to the doctor. And that we celebrated their birthdays."

Nur Ali listened and relayed all these conversations and observations back home to Shahgofta. He asked, "But you returned to Kabul in 1990?"

"Yes," replied Momen Khan. "When the Russians retreated, we joined the long caravans of refugees returning home."

"It was disastrous," added Shiriney. The roads were littered with mines. We saw so many kids missing limbs. It broke our hearts to see entire villages razed, fields and trees burned, and generally nothing to move back to."

"That's when we took everything we had and began the arduous journey to the US. And that was humiliating, too. I had to take work as a security guard when I was educated to be a lawyer ."

"And I worked in retail," added Shiriney.

"But at least we were here, safe and settled," Momen Khan often repeated in his narrations. "Over time, we were able to start the 7-Eleven franchise."

"You are a great success story," commented Nur Ali.

"Not really," retorted Momen Khan. "Our son, Adam, was born in America and is now in his last year of high school; he is struggling with identity issues and the social isolation that began with 9/11 for all us Muslims. In our attempt to raise him fully American, we didn't send Adam to to the mosque for religious education as did other Muslims, and we didn't encourage him to join the youth center there for activities and a sense of belonging. This was our mistake."

Adam came occasionally to the store, and Nur Ali had watched him grow up.

In addition to the ease and reliability in their relationship, Nur Ali also reported to Momen Khan and Shiriney the performance and reliability of other store employees. They relied on his advice, and he made recommendations both to hire and fire, perhaps unwittingly exercising his skill as family *qaida* in this new and alien context with non-family relations.

"Beware of anyone from south of the Malakand Pass," he would warn them about Punjabis in particular. "They're evil. They'll steal food and harm your store." And as he favored Pashtuns and Christians, they were mostly who worked in the store.

In the thirteen years he had worked seven nights a week for them, Nur Ali had always been paid in cash. He earned seven dollars an hour, five hundred eighty-eight per week for eighty-four hours. Momen Khan and Shiriney allowed him to keep his pay in a locked safe in the office, which he sent home regularly after paying his meager living expenses. He had no bank account or credit card and paid no taxes. And, upon occasion, if the bosses needed quick cash, they knew they could borrow from Nur Ali's stash in the safe.

When spats occasionally arose between Nur Ali and other employees over issues such as stealing donuts or cigarettes or insulting each other over religious matters and calling each other religious hypocrites, Shiriney invariably defended Nur Ali. "He's old and needs the money for his family," she would tell young coworkers who complained about him. "He's been exiled here fifteen years. Go apologize to him and try to get along."

PAKISTAN NOW

Tonight, Nur Ali called Shahgofta early in the evening, feeling punchy. "Salam alaykum," he began, assuming it was she who had picked up.

"Walaykum salam," she answered. She, too, had learned over the years, to immediately read the emotion in his voice, and could tell he was being playful. "Who are you looking for?"

"The insane," he replied.

"You have the wrong number," she continued playing along with him.

"Whose house is this?"

"Who is speaking?" Shahgofta was holding back her giggle behind an attempt to project authority.

"A lunatic."

"This is not the asylum."

"I thought it was the asylum."

"No, it certainly is not. If you're insane, you need to call the asylum." They both laughed heartily and then Shahgofta asked how he was.

"Passing time. The ground is below and the sky above. Are you the only one up? Everyone is sleeping? You just wait till I come home, and we'll see who sleeps all day! As for me, I may as well be in my grave. Thirteen years of standing on my feet twelve hours straight with no break, seven nights a week. My back hurts; my legs hurt; my head hurts! My arms burn from itching all the time." He knew it would solve nothing to complain, but he took comfort in her listening, and his face relaxed. His lower back pain came in cycles but seemed to intensify when he could voice it.

They each held their phones in silence a moment, content to hear the other's breathing, not needing to speak words. In an attempt to steer his thoughts away from his own pains and complaining, Nur Ali's mind shot back to a painless time of his life, and how his own mother had worked to make the hair braids despite the arthritis that ate at her fingers. Besides the baskets and other odds and ends, Nur Ali's father had also sold the braids made by the women of his house. Nur Ali occasionally teased Shahgofta, comparing her and her workload to his own mother's.

"She would sit on her low stool," he lectured his wife again tonight, "her black veil loose so as to show the red of her henna-stained hair and her round blue-framed glasses. She sat quiet, making the black and gold tassels woven into girls' braids. The bobbin of gold thread sat steady between her toes, as she pulled on the thread with her teeth to create tension and wove it around the black yarn with her hands. And when she wasn't busy with housework, she and my sister worked on the hair tassels and on decorated cords for swaddling infants. They embroidered flowers on sheets, pillow cases, and veils renowned in Swat. They never stopped."

"And you," Nur Ali addressed Shahgofta, "what do you do? You cook, you eat, and you sit idle while I, like my mother, agonize over here."

"Can't you take a pill?" she asked.

"I don't take pills. I don't believe in them. Besides, it's Rozha. Since when do we sacrifice the fast for a pill?"

"I live on pills all day when I'm not fasting," sighed Shahgofta.

"That's you. You're sick. I'm not sick. Besides," Nur Ali was particularly spirited tonight, "I have to tell you about my beard. You know I let it grow, and it's really long now. The boss wants me to shave it, but I refuse. Today, I was walking to work, and there was a man and woman walking a baby. Well, we were approaching each other from opposite directions, and as I came closer, the baby began to cry, and the closer we came to each other, the more frantic the crying became. When we actually crossed paths, the man told me it was my beard, that his child had never seen one so long, and that it had frightened her. Can you believe such a thing?"

Shahgofta laughed but suggested to her husband that maybe he should just cut his beard back some.

"Are you mad?" he cried out at her. "It's our religious duty, and I will not disrespect Allah by shaving or getting rid of it. Allah instructed us to wear it. The Prophet wore his, and no one told him to shave it. Allah sees everything, including my beard. It doesn't hurt me, and even if it does, let it! Let it grow!" Nur Ali placed a world of pride in his beard, and believed everyone else should also. Although the fashion among younger Pakistani men was now to shave all but a moustache, the older men of Swat had maintained the tradition of wearing beards, often dying them orange with henna to hide the gray.

"Has anyone in the house shaved their beard?" the *qaida* questioned his wife, naming each of his his close male relatives in turn . He periodically ran down a list of names, and she reported on each one as to the status of his beard. And later, when talking with them on the phone, he mentioned to them that he knew about their beard and teased the ones who had shaved.

Nur Ali related to Shahgofta all his dreams and nightmares, one of which concerned his beard. It was a recurring nightmare in which he woke up stripped of his treasured facial hair.

For some time now, coworkers had been complaining about Nur Ali's beard, suggesting to the bosses that it, along with the odors from his lack of bathing, and his constant scratching of bug bites, were turning customers away.

It was Shiriney who eventually gave him an ultimatum: "You either cut the beard back and bathe or I can't keep you on at the store."

"You know what our mullah said today at the mosque?" Nur Ali continued to Shahgofta, changing the subject, but still high pitched and agitated. This sudden lurch to a new topic was typical of their discontinuous conversations, of the announcement-driven dialogues created by distance and lack of intimacy. "He told us that as Muslims we couldn't use any other greeting other than 'salam alaykum,' which is Arabic. Like we use on the phone. You know how we Swatis say 'Don't be tired' in our own language to greet someone in person, and the person responds, 'Don't be poor.' Well, the mullah said we had to abandon all these greetings and use only the Arabic one to show our unity. I don't know what to think about that. It seems extreme."

"I don't think I could ever change the way I greet people to their face," replied Shahgofta, whose frown and shaking head Nur Ali could almost picture in his mind.

"Well, he's very serious about it. He said he didn't want to hear any more local greetings in anyone's individual language."

No call to Shahgofta went without asking if their older sons had called her from the ancestral home in the mountains where they remained in hiding with his brothers.

"Not today," she replied.

"What's wrong with them?" his voice mounted. "They have phones. If I can call from here, surely they can call, too, to check on their mother and wives!"

"Have there been any more disturbances in the village?" he asked, anxious for news to keep him informed.

"Nothing today. The hunger of fasting seems to keep everyone quiet."

Prodded by her husband's queries, Shahgofta dutifully reported every phone call and visit from every relative and neighbor she received, including what she served to the visitors, and what was spoken about during the visit. This superficially fed Nur Ali's insatiable hunger for knowledge about everything that happened in his house, even after fifteen years spent living half a world away from his home and family.

Of course, during Ramadan there were few visits to report. What was the point of visiting someone when there could be no tea and cookies? No weddings or celebrations ever took place during Ramadan. But the month of fasting was coming to an end, and preparations were being made for the holiday.

"I sent you money yesterday, in Na'im's name in the village. Make sure everyone gets clothes for the Eid holiday, and get bangles for the girls. A buffalo is more than we need, but we should be able to cover the price of two goats. See that it's distributed evenly among the neighbors and give a portion to the mosque for the poor. Divide the goat heads and the hooves among each of my three brothers' wives, but also include with it a fair portion of meat. And give our sons' wives enough to make good soup. And the girls should prepare enough rice to send a portion with each cut of meat. You all will be busy." Then he added, with a sigh, "I wish I could be there to see you in your new clothes."

"You know there is always a new suit of clothes waiting here for you, too," she tried in include him.

These religious holidays in exile were especially difficult moments for Nur Ali. He became obsessed with being in charge, with seeing that every dime he sent was spent appropriately to satisfy every need. From behind his 7-Eleven counter, he could imagine his nephews or cousins performing the ritual slaughter and cooking of the meat, while the women prepared giant pots of rice. He did take some comfort in knowing these religious holidays went on as they always had, in the open, and that people dressed up in clean or new clothes and performed the food-related visits and good cheer.

He thought of the pots of rice cooking over fires and could imagine each family member carefully mounding trays of rice to bury the bundles of cooked meat inside. It always made him smile to imagine the boys delivering the trays to various locations. Their sandaled feet ran quickly, quietly along the hillside and village paths as they held the trays and platters at head level. As *qaida,* Nur Ali agonized over the perfect performance of every detail, but his dream moments allowed him respite from back pain, itchy arms, and the drudgery of store tasks.

When his youngest daughter, Naseema, still at home and unmarried, got on the phone, Nur Ali ran down a long list of food items, asking the price of each one, so he could remain informed on things central to life there. And although Naseema never went to the bazar herself, she was intimately aware of item prices at each store. Rice, fat, sugar, tea, wheat, onions, tomatoes, salt, meat, and chicken were among the items whose price she could recite for her father, who could in turn always share the information with his compatriot exiles. And he knew what amount of the money he sent was being spent on food.

Naseema was just fourteen, studying through correspondence, as so many girls did after a certain age. She had attended the girls' government school in the village through fifth grade, clad in white pants and a sky-blue dress, the standard uniform for all school girls in Pakistan. There, she had learned her letters and numbers, and could at least write or read off a telephone number or write down a money order number when her father needed her to do so. Raised in the family compound by her mother, aunts, and uncles, she had never known much beyond that life.

Naseema's older sister, Shahgul, was married and gone, so she and her sisters-in-law, Rabia and Sher Banu, were now the only ones to look after her aging mother and assume the household chores. Naseema was quiet and subservient, performing her endless list of tasks, without too much thought as to what the future held, apart from an eventual marriage, a transference of her workload and subservience from her mother to a mother-in-law. Of this she had no doubt, as her mother now had two daughters-in-law to do her work, and her marriage would entail a financial reward for her parents.

"You just attend to your lessons, and pay special attention to your math," the *qaida* counseled the daughter he barely knew, "so you can manage your family finances and business one day."

"You won't ever sell me to an unknown Arab for the highest bid, or anything like that, will you?" the girl asked her father. "I've had a few friends sold off in hard times, and it's talked about throughout Swat."

"Goodness, girl," Nur Ali's voice rose angrily into the receiver. "We don't do things like that in our family. We may experience hard times, but we stick together as a family. Don't let me hear you talk like that again."

"I know, Qaidada," replied Naseema. "My sisters-in-law are so fortunate to have married into a pleasant household like ours where everyone gets along."

"You tell them that," interrupted Nur Ali.

"It's just that there are so many horror stories of girls finding themselves with abusive mothers-in-law who worked them to excess, or sisters-in-law who, driven by jealousy, slander the newcomer alleging crimes of infidelity in order to have her stoned or driven from the house. We girls all exchange stories of young wives being mistreated or burned to death by their in-laws who dislike them."

"Your mother and I will never let anything like that happen to you," he reassured the girl listening to his voice. "We would never put you in such a situation."

"I believe you, Qaidada," responded Naseema.

"Meanwhile, however," he instructed the child, you remain at home with your mother, and always behave with modesty. In our house, women belong at home, and not out in public, or unveiled. There is a young female Moroccan worker here, Layla. She is very decent. She is Muslim, and I call her 'Sister,' as I do all the female Muslims who come into the store veiled."

The strong adherence to women's public veiling or sequestering, Nur Ali believed, was what distinguished Swat Pashtuns from other Pakistanis, and what so outraged him whenever the family reported another house raid by soldiers looking for Taliban sympathizers. He perceived these government soldiers as invading the sanctity of home privacy, where women were kept hidden from unrelated men, and he felt incapable of protecting and guaranteeing that sanctity. Pashtuns respected it among themselves and never entered another's home. If men visited each other, they remained in the space designated for outsiders, and they were entertained and fed there, separate from the family space. Nur Ali was especially guarded when it came to his last and youngest daughter, and he kept a vigilant eye on her.

Despite his strong belief in gender separation, Nur Ali repeatedly told Shahgofta during their conversations that there was no modesty required with one's own husband. Veiling, modesty, and subservience were expected of Pashtun women toward men, but Nur Ali encouraged Shahgofta to interact openly with him, and she often did so.

"You know, we are married. And once we are married and in private, no modesty is required." He envied the open relationships between American men and women he saw on television or even sometimes in the store and wished he could get his own wife to act this way with him.

"I know," his wife replied. "But you can't see that when you talk with me, I am often surrounded by other people and cannot talk freely with you."

Even at home, they had only ever been equals together in private or when walking in the mountains far from the eyes of Khwaza Khel. It was rumored that a woman could be as bold as they wanted as long as they did it hidden from those most likely to create scandal.

"Is it sunny in the courtyard today?" asked Nur Ali, his mind slipping away nostalgically to his home as he had left it. The family compound did not sit in the bazaar of Khwaza Khel, but a short walk up the mountain from there following narrow foot paths. Mud walls enclosed a spacious courtyard surrounded by a covered verandah and rooms that opened onto it. The large enclosed courtyard, invisible from outside, was home to chickens, to the family buffalo, and was where the women spent the day engaged in various activities in the open air and warm sun. The thought of the women enjoying the sun inside this space brought a smile to his lips.

"What color veil are you wearing today? And is your hair showing?" his voice lowered. He smiled as he heard her whispered reply.

"Yes." Inside the courtyard, women could drop their heavy veils and don their light house veil, even allowing it to drop off their head when engaged in tasks. Of course, the sound of the call for prayer that echoed uphill from Khwaza Khel routinely reminded them to pull the veil back up over their heads in an unthinking gesture he could picture. *The call to righteousness,* he thought. *The recall to propriety.*

Their outhouse was an enclosure built right on a stream that ran down into the main river, so no one needed to carry around the spouted container to cleanse themselves. Theirs was the cleanest, odor-free toilet in all of Swat, he always thought. In this private compound, husbands could interact with wives, and families could interact together as such. It was a sacred place of intimacy, love, and nurturing, as well as it was home to the family bickering that never left its walls.

"Tell me what's going on in the courtyard right now," he pleaded.

Obediently, Shahgofta described the scene. "The girls have just filled the water pots, and are busy sweeping off the verandah. The little ones are chasing the chickens around." In his 7-Eleven, the exile pictured the twelve round clay pots of water kept in the shade of the courtyard, each one capped with a flat-bottomed tin bowl to protect the water from bugs and dust, and to function as a drinking vessel. If he closed his eyes he could almost smell the earthy odor of the water.

The courtyard had several twine cots, which were continually dragged from the sunny courtyard to the surrounding verandah in case of rain or excessive heat. Unlike their Afghan neighbors, residents of Swat did not sit on carpets, but on cots and low stools strung with twine and sinew, which could be moved from sun to shade, depending on the season and desire. Two wooden cradles hung from ceiling beams for swinging babies to sleep, and a large wooden open shelving unit served to store and display the household aluminum plates and serving trays, as well as the colorful china tea cups.

The 7-Eleven employee smiled as he recalled the shiny décor.

"Are you sitting in the sun on one of the cots?"

"Yes, the sun is warm today."

As a child, Nur Ali had grown up in the compound with his parents, his uncles, their wives, and all his paternal cousins. Each nuclear family occupied its own room, tight as it was, with the children and parents doubled up, head to foot on the twine-strung cots, and metal trunks filled with clothes stacked neatly and covered with embroidered fabrics. As a young father, Nur Ali had shared a bed with their son, while Shahgofta slept with their daughter.

"I suppose the guest room is not being used too much these days. Are you keeping it free of dust and flies?"

"It's always ready for guests," Shahgofta replied.

Outside the compound, but adjoining the outer wall, was a separate room containing a few cots covered with embroidered sheets and cushions. This was the space reserved for entertaining male guests who could not enter the compound, typical of most Pashtun homesboth urban and rural. Unconcerned with concealment, this room had its own small open verandah from which, in his mind now, Nur Ali looked out over the green mountains and down into the river valley. He had learned the tradition of entertaining as a child from his father, for whom he often shuttled plates and cups as his father sat discussing matters with guests. When his father did not have him running errands, Nur Ali had been allowed to sit in the shadows, unobserved, absorbing the behavior. Before he had left, Nur Ali himself and his brothers had often entertained in the guest quarters.

"You know I always report any visits to you. I tell you how long they stay, what we serve them, and what gifts they bring, if any."

Their conversation was brought to an abrupt haltby a signal that the minutes had expired.

7-ELEVEN

"Hello, 7-Eleven," Nur Ali answered the phone.

It was Bacha Gul.

"Salam alaykum, Brother, how are you?" queried his friend. Following etiquette, even friends did not address each other by name, but by a kinship title, and these two had adopted "Brother" to show their close male peer relationship.

"What can I say, Brother?" replied Nur Ali. "Time passes by, and I am passing the time. We're all outsiders, all exiles, all living the same existence and passing the time."

No matter how frustrated or upset Nur Ali ever was with things at his own home, he never shared a breath of it with any of his exiled acquaintances beyond his horrified response to the political situation at large or to the news of life losses . Even after a call home left him moaning with tears, or trembling with rage, if a friend called to see how he was doing, he would gather his composure, and his response was always the same: "Time is passing," he would say steadily, "and we're all passing time here in exile. All is good."

No one pressed him for more: There was an unspoken rule in being Pashtun—even called "doing" Pashto—that one should never reveal emotions or personal feelings, or discuss private family matters with anyone unrelated. And Nur Ali, as deeply steeped in his culture as he was, abided by this.

Most of Nur Ali and Bacha Gul's conversations centered on comparing what news they had heard from their home villages, and who was doing what in the exiled Pashtun community.

"Have you called home recently?" queried Nur Ali.

"Why?" replied Bacha Gul. "Do you know something I don't know? It's Rozha. We know what's going on at home."

"Still, you need to call more often. Who knows if someone's been hurt, or your house needs repairs. You should make sure that everyone is alright."

"Actually," started Bacha Gul, "I was calling you to ask what is the official time to break our fast."

Nur Ali was recognized in the community not only as an old man, a resource for jobs and housing for newly arrived Pashtuns, but as an authority on Islam and matters such as this. And he took pride in the recognition he was given for his religious expertise, as well as for his knowledge of current news from home, and for the close ties he kept with his family. He was undeniably a respected elder in the Pashtun immigrant community.

"Before you see daylight," the night manager informed his friend. But he had other news to share tonight. "Listen, did you hear about the bus in Mingora, and the three boys shot right there in the middle of the bazaar?"

"I heard it mentioned, but without any details," answered Bacha Gul.

"Do you know anything about who they were?"

"One of the guys," began Nur Ali, "was the grandson of a midwife from a village close to mine. I'll tell you if I hear anything more. I swear, we have nothing left. Our homes are destroyed, our families dispersed. There are no men to look after the women or farm the fields. We have nothing left, and yet they still come after us."

Anger subsided as Nur Ali listened to Bacha Gul chatting away. He didn't hear the words, but instead pictured his own father in their village shop, the way he had seen him so many years. In his small shop in the Khwaza Khel market, Nur Ali's father had sold candies, tea, sugar, sewing supplies, their own fruit, wheat, and other necessities and luxuries he could acquire. Clients came to him from other villages as he was reputed to have the best baskets that men strapped onto donkeys to transport goods through the mountains to villages not serviced by a road. Like most men in Swat, he dyed his beard red with henna, darkened his eyes with antimony, and wore the local brown wool hat, pancake flat on his heat with the edge rolled. Lying back on cushions with his legs crossed, he looked much like most shopkeepers in the village, just waiting for business.

The thought of his father sitting in his shop produced a thin smile on Nur Ali's lips as Bacha Gul's voice brought him back from his reverie, with some local news to contribute. "Hey, did you hear me? You know Moambar, the one who worked the food cart?"

"Yeah," Nur Ali knew every Swati in the city and had helped many of them find jobs and housing upon their arrival. "He was from Imam Derrai and worked here with me for a while. But when his cousin arrived, they started to work a food cart together. What about him?"

"His wife and kids were living in an apartment in Karachi, where someone broke in and shot them all dead. Just like that! He's devastated. The community is all pitching in and getting him a ticket, so he can fly home."

"What awful Godless times we live in! Of course, I'll contribute." Scratching his arm Nur Ali added, as if to rub salt into the painful story, "Can you believe Moambar used to have a thriving cement business back home? He had accumulated a fortune, and then lost it all from one day to the next when the Bearded Ones came and confiscated it. And now this! Our people

just don't ever get a break." He ran his hand over the gray strands that covered his forehead, and then on down through his beard and thought, *This could be happening to any one of us here.*

As if to add to their mounting despair, Nur Ali questioned Bacha Gol: "I heard about Naveed who came here recently from Mingora to escape the Taliban."

"Yes," replied Bacha Gol. "He belonged to some peace committee in Swat, where he and his relatives were constantly being harassed and persecuted by the Taliban. His family was threatened. The authorities picked him up the other day and wanted to deport him far from Swat to Karachi but an American expert testified that he would not be able to remain anonymous in Karachi. The judge allowed him to stay for now."

"Yes, but for how long?" responded Nur Ali. "As long as he stays here, he will constantly be looking over his shoulder, afraid to move for fear the authorities will send him back."

"What can we do?" His friend was eager to change the subject and turned to their usual reminiscing about Swat. What could they accomplish by extending the list of these stories? Nothing positive to help them survive. "How is your *naswar* supply, Brother? Do you ever think back to our hashish-smoking days in the village?"

"Sure," replied Nur Ali, his voice calm again. The continued pain in his back was dull and, suddenly relaxing into his fatigue, he reached his hand to press down on it, now an unwitting daily reflex. "I used to go late at night to the back room of our kabob house in Khwaza Khel," he said wistfully as the pain dissipated in his back. "The few light beams entering the place were so thick with smoke and dust it made our eyes tear."

"I don't regret that part," laughed Bacha Gul, grateful that he and his friend were back onto good memories, and laughing over them.

"And we'd sit on our heels in the shadows, continued Nur Ali. "We'd hold that breath as long as we could, and then spit out the water onto the floor. If there were enough of us in the room, all you could see was smoke and spewing water." He was laughing hard now.

"Some guys couldn't hold it," added Bacha Gol with a chuckle, "or ended up spitting and coughing uncontrollably, retreating from our circle onto a cot, head between their knees and coughing and spitting down to their feet. You knew it was over when they finally wiped their eyes, nose and mouth with their shirt bottom. I remember those days," he sighed with a giggle

"Yes," agreed Nur Ali, "it seems a life time ago. We sure were careless mountain boys back then. Now we worry about back pain and our families."

Having forgotten the answer to his original query, Bacha Gul again asked what time he should eat his breakfast before the official fast began.

"If you finish eating by five, you should be alright," advised Nur Ali. "I'll call you later. I have a crowd to take care of." Many of Nur Ali's conversations ended this way, when the number of customers overcame his skill for juggling them with phone calls.

PAKISTAN BEFORE

Nur Ali was twenty-five when he began working as a crewman on a cargo ship. After his father had appointed him to leave Swat and go seek income elsewhere, he had gone to the Karachi shipyards where he found they were hiring. Relatives helped him obtain a passport and seaman's papers, and he was hired very quickly to clean, assist in the engine room, run errands onboard, and join the longshoremen in loading and unloading when in port. Most of his coworkers were not Pashtun, so he learned to speak broken Urdu, which he had never had to use much in Swat. It was clearly not his native language, and he became known among his colleagues as the "Wild Pathan." Many non-Pashtuns in Pakistan feared Pashtuns for their reputation as fearless mountain warriors and armed tribesmen. They referred to them using the British term "Pathan." Pashtuns were stereotyped for kidnapping people and keeping them in the tribal area where no one could pursue them. They had also, in the 1980s and 1990s, gained the reputation of selling their daughters to wealthy Arabs for healthy sums of money. And after 9/11, the very name Pashtun became associated in the global media with the Taliban. Nur Ali enjoyed educating his shipmates regarding his native Swat Valley. They were peaceful farmers and shopkeepers, and had never been warriors, unlike their tribal counterparts.

Working on the ship for ten years, Nur Ali traveled to ports all over the world . He sent money home regularly and returned home on leave every twenty-three months for one month. These homecomings were always sweet, a time to bond with his children and enjoy making more children with Shahgofta. When he was feeling melancholy standing alone behind the 7-Eleven counter he would think back to the last night he had been home in Khwaza Khel before embarking on what he did not know would turn into a fifteen-year absence.

That night, as every last night before the *qaida* left on tour, Shahgofta and her sisters-in-law prepared a special dinner with rice and buffalo meat stew, along with sautéed curried peppers, Nur Ali's favorite. He watched his wife as she, from her low stool, held the carving knife upright between her feet and slid the chunk of meat he had brought home up and down the blade to slice appropriate size pieces for stew. Although he had observed this gesture hundreds of times, performed by his mother and all the other women of the household, he watched attentively that night, letting it lodge permanently in his mind's video recorder, to conjure up on lonely nights on the ship.

With the same reflection he listened to the sounds of dough that Lawangina was slapping from one palm to the next before smacking it down against the tandur wall. As he sat memorizing each one's face, with his sons Ahmad and Iqbal close by, he inhaled the bitter smell of smoke that rose from the wood cooking fires and hovered over them. After dinner and prayers, the family sat together in the courtyard. Nur Ali read excerpts from the Quran while Shahgofta combed through his mother's hair with meticulous fingers searching for lice and other scalp crud. She then braided Bibi's hair, still orange from the last time she had applied henna. And lying next to his wife that night, he deeply inhaled the smell of fire smoke that clung to her clothing, her hair. Nur Ali wondered when he would see, smell, hear, and taste this scene again. He would retain, with the distance, the memory of flesh on the outside of his telephone interlocutor, but the unknown feelings on the inside, hidden behind the nose crinkles, smiles, frowns, and other indicators, he would be blind to.

It wasn't until his ship was docked in Savannah, however, that Nur Ali was approached by a shipmate.

"Come on, Pathan. We can do this. We'll stay in America, find jobs, and really make some money. You have four children, don't you?"

"Yes," slowly replied Nur Ali. "And a fifth one on the way. But I don't know. I don't have anyone here."

"I do," replied his friend confidently. "I have a cousin in Florida. He'll get us started. I don't think that's too far from here."

"But can we still go back home?" Nur Ali was still hesitant.

"After we get settled here, sure."

"And how do we settle here?

"It's easy," his friend encouraged Nur Ali. "My cousin will help us make local ID cards to get started. You can also pay someone to marry you and get citizenship that way. Then you separate and go your own way. There are lots of options. You can start a life in America and make lots of money to send home, more than you do with this job, you can also save for your retirement."

"No second wife for me. I like the notion of remaining in America to work and send money to support my family at home, but nothing will make me take a second wife. It's perfectly legal and accepted at home, and I know many men who thought they could resolve their marital issues by taking a second wife. But I've only ever seen their issues doubled. I swore I would never do it." He had once misunderstood his sister's husband to be taking a second wife, and he raged furiously at Shahgofta about this shameless practice that left a first wife outcast and neglected.

"But you've convinced me. Let's stay in America!"

That night, waiting for a bus in the Savannah depot, Nur Ali bought a phone card and placed a call home. He announced his news to a speechless Shahgofta, adding that he would send home good money, but did not know when he could return.

The crewman's cousin helped Nur Ali get an ID card, and with the money he had, the new exile traveled north to Washington DC where he learned he had a distant relative. He remained there several months, trying out one odd job after another, but nothing seemed to work out for him. He didn't drive and had not learned any technical skills during his years at sea.

After he had been in the country two years, traveling throughout the northeast from one connection to another, he finally met Momen Khan and his wife, Shiriney, the Afghans who owned a couple of 7-Elevens where the turn-over was rapid fire. Nur Ali started working there at once, alongside Matthew who painstakingly taught him each store-related task, including the stock phrases he would use from behind the cash register. The exile struggled with the pronuncition of these, and Matthew repeated without ever raising his voice. It was Shiriney who trusted Nur Ali and made him night manager after a few short months.

For housing, he started out renting a room in a house with a prominent Pashtun, Khan, who was putting his sons through medical school. But he argued with them over prayers, financial, and food issues, and he finally moved on to an apartment shared by two Baluchis and a Panjabi from other provinces of Pakistan. Now it was just four of them.

Throughout this time he never acquired any technical skills, and had no appreciation or need for computers. Had he learned about computers, he would undoubtedly have joined the throngs of immigrants who communicated with home using video calls over the internet. But Nur Ali never experienced this. He ran his entire life from and through the 7-Eleven.

7-ELEVEN

Nur Ali's life at the 7-Eleven presented not only a link with home via the telephone, but human contacts with other exiles and Americans with whom he shared daily experiences. The store comprised an important part of his life, and he spoke about his co-workers to Shahgofta. He got along particularly well with Pashto speaking Christians, which explained why so many worked there. They differed from him in that they were seeking asylum in America from religious persecution at home. There was Samuel, who spent his time pursuing Hispanic girlfriends. He called them with persistence to profess his love and invite himself over after his shift. This disgusted Nur Ali, who stood by in silence to witness what he could hear of these conversations, but never spoke against Samuel. The efforts tended to end in frustration, in any case. "I can come after work, and you can have dinner for me?" he would ask one potential girlfriend after another, but these requests were usually turned down, leaving poor Samuel to return, sullen, to his store tasks.

Samuel alternated with Michael, so that one of these two usually worked until midnight with Nur Ali, when the store was most likely to be the target of late night robberies. Michael was more afraid of the resulting conversations with the police than of the criminals themselves and begged Nur Ali to handle these. Michael lived in fear of deportation. He had always lived on the defensive as a Christian in a Muslim country. More critically, of late, as his and his family's safety was no longer guaranteed back home with the increased violence and church burnings by the Taliban. The fact that his asylum status was still pending made matters worse. Michael's plight gave Nur Ali a broader perspective. He realized that however precarious his own status was, there was someone worse off.

And then there was Matthew, another Pashto-speaking Christian from Peshawar, who worked the earlier portion of the night shift for three years with Nur Ali, during which they had become good friends . They worked well together, and it was Matthew who had taught Nur Ali how to perform many of his tasks at the store. But he had moved on to a fried chicken take-out closer to home when his family immigrated to the US to join him. Considerably younger than Nur Ali and hence addressing him as "Mama" (Uncle) or "Lala" (Older Brother), Matthew still called each evening so they could compare stories of their workplaces and of other Pashtuns they knew in the city. He was Nur Ali's go-to person for questions concerning store issues or technical problems like jams in the receipt dispenser.

Another coworker, Sherry, was the elderly American lady from down the street, born, raised, and married in the same neighborhood. She only worked day shifts, and spent hours tending what she claimed as her own displays by the counter. She was particularly attentive to the candy display. Even when she wasn't working, she came into the store to arrange and place orders for her candy display, to purchase lottery tickets or special sale items, or just to get a cup of coffee. She played mother hen to the young men, all of whom were foreign to her local culture. She would never understand their needs and frustrations, their lives, or their fears, but the store was home to her in many ways. And they, in turn, at times resented her nagging interference and gossiped about her mannerisms and cigarette smoking, but they tolerated her mothering advice. She had worked at the 7-Eleven under the previous franchisees and had pleaded with Momen Khan and Shiriney to let her stay. And in reality, she played a huge role in getting them started there.

Ironically, Sherry was distinctly different from the other employees merely by being American. She shared no element of the store culture, but apart from indicating by a mere "What?" that she didn't understand what they said, she never expressed any surprise or interest in how they behaved, nor compared them to herself. She enjoyed working mornings alongside Layla, the Moroccan girl. And although Sherry was never made a manager, she looked over the store as if she owned it. She called the store eight to twelve times a day if she was off, and when she was working, called the boss every hour to report some detail or other about the store or employees. Sherry had been at the store since it opened, and although she and Nur Ali worked different shifts and rarely crossed paths, she occasionally called him with advice about an order, a piece of machinery that needed attention, or the candy display.

Sherry was the only person there who addressed Nur Ali by name. One night she called him with some directives for switching the gum and the breath mints, and Samuel answered her call.

"Put Nur Ali on the phone," she asked.

And Samuel, who was a new employee and who had never heard his coworker named other than 'Kaka,' replied, "There's no one here by that name."

"He's right there. I can hear him talking next to you," Sherry insisted.

"The guy with the beard!"

Samuel laughed as he realized who she was referring to and turned to Nur Ali. "Kaka, it's Sherry for you."

Another employee was Mo, the loud Moroccan who made everyone laugh between his crude humor and thick accent. Considering himself a ladies' man, he advised Samuel to be more forceful in his approach to dating, and he offered cultural advice.

"Ask how she is," Mo counseled Samuel. "Talk on the phone about what she does and doesn't like. And don't invite yourself over for dinner with someone you barely know. American girls don't like that."

Mo floated from store to store until he was fired for his overly aggressive jocularity with customers and fellow employees. After Shiriney fired him, he occasionally called Nur Ali and Michael from his new store to chat and keep them company and make them laugh at his crude jokes and American jargon imitations: "Hey, Mudda Fucka! How you doin' Mudda Fucka? You busy over there?"

Michael would laugh along and mimic him: "No, Mudda Fucka! Not much goin' on here."

And Layla, the young Moroccan who worked days with Sherry, was married to a taxi driver. She worked regularly and came in with Sherry to relieve Nur Ali at seven each morning. Nur Ali once told Shahgofta that he regarded Layla as his own youngest daughter, Naseema.

"She wears a veil and is quiet and discreet," he told his wife. As he was a firm believer in exiles calling home and in children calling their parents, he occasionally offered Layla his phone card when she arrived in the morning, if it had minutes left on it, to call her mother. She was young, and Nur Ali felt compelled to act like a father toward her.

Layla took care of cash reports and walked to the bank twice per shift to deposit the cash from the register. She, along with the bosses, scheduled the employees and handled the payroll. She was young, attentive to detail, and meticulous about the store's appearance. She never raised her voice and treated everyone alike. But she did not appreciate Mo's outspokenness, and she referred to him as that "bad guy" or "gangster." Nur Ali protected her from Mo's indiscretions.

The employees were all connected to some extent, and although the younger employees treated Nur Ali with the respect due his age, they didn't hesitate to criticize him harshly to the bosses.

"He shows anger at the customers," Michael once reported when Shiriney asked. "He swears at them and says he hates these people. He calls them names."

"He doesn't wash, and he smells bad," Sherry told Shiriney another time. "His beard is straggly and offensive. And he's always scratching his arms like he has fleas!"

Occasionally, Nur Ali's coworkers even went so far as to apologize to customers for him, attempting to explain that his beard was a religious symbol and he was an old man.

As coworkers, however, the group cooperated and knew they had to keep the store afloat as a team, and they generally managed to do so. They also came to each other's support when customers assaulted them with racial and ethnic slurs, addressing them as "Muslim terrorists," or worse.

PAKISTAN NOW

"Salam alaykum."

"Walaykum salam." It was Sher Banu, Nur Ali's daughter-in-law, who picked up the phone today. Shahgofta had announced to her husband the day before that their daughter-in-law was expecting a second child.

"How are you? I've been trying to get through for hours, but no one ever picks up."

"We're well, God willing, Qaidada."

"That's good." Without losing a breath, or questioning the tone behind her voice, the qaida went on to lecture the young woman about Allah and the need to remain faithful and solid in their prayers. Having been gone so many years, lecturing had become the only way he knew to communicate with his children and grandchildren. How could he feel intimacy with a being he had never touched? A few passing, brief moments on the phone with most individuals was his only contact with them. And even in these fleeting moments, he had so much to impart to them, so much to review and instruct, that this one-sided practical lecturing had become his only channel for communication. It was void of the typical eye-to-eye exchanges most humans enjoy, things like the knowing glance to signal mutual feeling, or the smiling or twinkling eye that could soften even the harshest words. His words were void of any physical sharing like discreet hand or knee touching in moments of closeness, patting a son on the shoulder to show concern or admiration, or proudly holding a child in his arms as he walked through the bazaar. He knew all this, missed all this, but carried on as if his life depended on pushing it aside.

"Nazia has an earache and has been crying for two days now," said Sher Banu when it came her turn to give her full report. "Naser went to the village to get some aspirin, and returned with antibiotic powder, but I worry about her."

As she explained the problem and what they had been doing to resolve it, Nur Ali's head was already racing; he also felt a knot growing in his stomach. Although he had been gone fifteen years, and was half a world away, the fact remained that he was *qaida,* and with his brothers and sons away from home, he was responsible for his sisters-in-law, his daughters-in-law, and now his granddaughter.

I will find a way... I have to, Nur Ali thought. It was his duty now—at four o'clock in the morning from behind his 7-Eleven counter—to find a solution and get medical attention for his granddaughter in the mountains of Swat. He felt especially driven by responsibility toward Sher Banu, whose husband was being hounded and may never legally return home. In order to do this, he had to first find a male escort for the young mother, so she could take her daughter to the local doctor in Khwaza Khel, Mingora, or even to the hospital in Peshawar if necessary.

Sher Banu passed the phone to Shahgofta and he spoke with her to brainstorm solutions, suggesting one male relative after another for the task.

"Why can't Naser escort her?" questioned Shahgofta.

"He's already been stopped and questioned by the authorities. He's still young, and we don't need to put him in a situation," the *qaida* had the last word.

"Maybe her husband could come down from the mountain and take care of his own wife and daughter," suggested Shahgofta with sarcasm.

"You know that can't happen. Do you want see him caught and thrown in jail?" Nur Ali snapped.

"Well, your brothers won't come and do anything. It's as though they don't want to be associated with us, as if we're responsible for them having to hide from their own home. Mahmad Ali has instructed Sabina not to let their sons be seen publicly with us. So they can't escort her."

"That's enough. I would take the girl myself if I weren't so far away."

"Yeah, like you can just hop on a plane and rush home every time there's an emergency. Naser got her some medicine. The child should be fine. We've all dealt with sick children before."

But the knot in Nur Ali's stomach would not loosen until he personally found a solution. He was determined to have the child examined by a proper doctor, and the only way to accomplish this was to have the mother and child escorted somewhere. And he was the only person who could coordinate this.

"There's my cousin, Akbar Ali, right there in Khwaza Khel," suggested Nur Ali.

"I don't want any favors from them," retorted Shahgofta. "His wife never came to either of your parents' funerals. I broke ties with them."

Nur Ali had decided, however, and there was no arguing. He hung up and immediately called Akbar Ali. "Salam alaykum." The knot in his stomach was replaced now with a drive to simply resolve an issue. *Just tackle it and it will get done.*

"Walaykum salam. Who is calling?"

"It's me, your cousin in America," replied Nur Ali. He heard a police siren sounding off in the street outside and watched its lights as they flashed by the door. A man entered, took a coca cola from the cooler, and laid it on the counter. Nur Ali followed him with his eyes.

"Lala, how are you?" asked his cousin, sounding surprised.

"Will that be all?" the night manager recited the words to his customer, his voice suddenly very soft. "One twenty-nine."

The customer put down the exact change and proceeded out the door.

"Is that you, Lala? How are you?" repeated his cousin, somewhat confused by the other conversation.

"I'm fine. But I need you to do something for me. My granddaughter is sick and needs to see a doctor. We have no one at home right now to escort her mother. You need to go with her." Nur Ali was careful, as always, never to mention his son or any women by name. "You can see the doctor in Khwaza Khel, and then pick up whatever medication they need. Her mother will have bus fare in case you need to take them to Mingora."

"Of course," agreed his cousin. "You're in need and there's no man in the house. It's my honor to help out ."

Once he had confirmed an escort, Nur Ali called the house back to inform Sher Banu of the plan he had put in place.

"Thank you, Qaidada. That's a great relief," replied his daughter-in-law, on the verge of tears. He heard the despair and relief in her voice. What choice did he have? A strange, fierce determination made him stronger than he was and led him to do what was needed to keep home life in order. That projected strength in turn gave his wife and other women of the house the faith to continue to hold him up as provider and head of the family.

"And don't you worry about doctor fees or bus fare if you have to go Mingora. I'll be sending money soon." The *qaida* was unaware that the 7-Eleven phone was bugged and that every money order he sent home was being recorded by the authorities as added evidence of his terrorist support. Nur Ali then changed his tone. "Does your husband call you?"

Sher Banu sensed that her father-in-law was baiting her to complain about her husband, and replied respectfully, "Yes, *Qaidada*, but it's not safe for him to be seen in the village."

There was nothing more to say, and Nur Ali asked her to put Bibi back on, meaning Shahgofta, who now sounded tired and frail. "Salam alaykum."

Somewhat relieved of the pressure and trying to steady the tone of his voice if not the knot in his stomach, Nur Ali started by raging at his wife over the absurdity of the situation. "How can this happen to us? My own grandchild's useless father, our son, is incapable of fulfilling his family obligations. A man's only legitimate concerns in life should be his parents, his wife and children, and his brothers and sisters. Beyond caring for his family," he ranted, "a man has no purpose in life."

Once he had let off this steam, pressing into his lower back with his hand, Nur Ali began his conversation with the usual litany of questions: "How's your headache? Have the boys called? Any news from anyone?"

Shahgofta had barely started to answer, and Nur Ali was now intently listening to her, trying to pick out vocal indications of sarcasm, fear, hope, anything, when there was a sudden commotion in the store. From her end, Shahgofta heard a door open with a crash, quick footsteps, the voice of a frantic woman. She then heard her husband speak in English. By now she was accustomed to him holding double conversations, with her on the one hand, and with customers on the other. She didn't understand the English but waited for him to address her again.

"I call the cops," she heard her husband say. "You wait. Police is coming. I close store." Nur Ali addressed a young woman who had tumbled into the store, seemingly inebriated.

"They're all after me," she cried, "my boyfriend and the other guys. They mad at me. They going to hurt me. You gotta help me! Don't let them get me!" The young woman was in distress and seemed somewhat pacified by this straggly, bearded Muslim who was offering to help her.

Having worked the night shift in a bad section of the city for thirteen years, Nur Ali was used to this kind of situation, and methodically went through the steps. "You need to use the phone?" He always allowed people in need to use the store phone. Victims of theft or abuse called the police, teens on drugs called their parents in tears to come get them, women called for protection from abusive boyfriends, men called women for a reminder of what it was they had been sent to buy. Nur Ali himself called 9-1-1 one to three times a week to report homeless, injured, or aggressive people, petty thieves, major thefts at gun point, drug overdoses, or other sources of aggravation for the store. The girl shook her head no and appeared satisfied to remain safely hidden inside the store for a while.

"The bitch comes in here and wants my help," Nur Ali resumed his conversation with Shahgofta. "What am I supposed to do?"

"Let her own husband take care of her."

"He's not here. He's home drunk, like everyone else around here. They drink at night, lose their heads, and piss their pants. They're all drunks in this country. And she's out with other men. Damn them all to hell!" He now entirely ignored the woman in the store and went into a rant. "You know what the Prophet, and what Allah himself prescribed in this regard?" Nur Ali often preached religious anecdotes to his wife, while she listened dutifully. "They said it right there in the Quran, that if a man looks at a woman, she must lower her eyes. And a woman has no business looking at any unrelated male. And if a man has to go to a relative's house, he must first call out and knock on the door to announce himself and check if there are men in the house. And if there are none, he may not enter. A woman can talk from behind the door, but the man cannot see as much as her clothing. Those are Allah's orders to Muslims. Obey them or go to Hell!" His apparent coldness was no more than practical enumeration of rules. He resorted to the lecture mode of communication brought on by distance and lack of connectedness.

The young woman stood aside, staring bewildered at the garrulous bearded man who yelled fast and harshly into the phone in a language strange to her. Feeling ignored, and secure that she had escaped harm, she slipped out of the store while the *qaida* pursued his telephone conversation. And he, engrossed in far more important matters, never gave her another thought.

Shahgofta, a little more understanding, explained, "There are women here, in our cities, who walk unveiled in the bazaar! If they're informed, then they are responsible for their behavior, but there are people who are just plain ignorant, who have not learned the way of the Prophet. Their crime is one of not attempting to be informed. That's what our mullah here says."

As with most calls home, Nur Ali next went on to speak with everyone and checked on them all. Now that he had resolved Sher Banu's issue, he knew it would arouse the others' envy if he did not address them all. After speaking with Shahgofta and Sabina, he exchanged greetings with his two other sisters-in-law, Lawangina and Salma. They each in turn told him stories of violence and abuse in the village conducted by Pakistani army soldiers.

"Yesterday," Salma spoke at full speed, "they chopped down the family fruit trees in the orchard and, after cutting and bundling the small wood for their own needs, they dragged the tree trunks into the fields, ruining the rice crop that was beginning to come in."

Lawangina took over with the narrative, equally out of breath. "They did this in an attempt to put pressure on the women to reveal where all the men have fled."

Nur Ali remained riveted to the phone, taking in every word, gasping in disbelief but not interrupting. His heart emptied and as he listened and digested each item, each emotion spilling from the phone receiver into his ear. *I need to maintain control. This needs to be made right. I have to make it right.*

"The dogs even destroyed the bicycle which Lawangina's son left standing outside the compound wall when he came home for lunch," added Salma.

And the worst news of all, which sent Nur Ali's very core writhing with anger, was that just this morning the soldiers had stormed their compound, as well as several others, in search of papers, letters, passports, and identity documents leading to information on the missing household men. He could feel the pain in his back soar, and immediately he felt a need to scratch his itchy arms.

"Allah!" cried out Nur Ali upon hearing the news. "Do those dogs have no mothers and sisters of their own? Are they even Muslim anymore? Have they never heard of shame or discretion?"

Although he knew the soldiers were primarily searching for Iqbal as a Taliban sympathizer, he also suspected they were after him personally because he was sending money home, ostensibly supporting the criminal, and that the Pakistani government had reported him to the US authorities. Shahgofta had once informed him that the soldiers had circulated a list of names of wanted people and that his name had been on it. If this were the case, then he along with his wife and children were endangering the rest of the family as his brother had suggested. He also knew this meant he was likely to be deported from America, where immigrants with a criminal record in their own country were now being deported. Samuel had informed him that two American men wearing suits had come in asking for him by name during the day shift.

I will find a way. I have to.

"Listen," Nur Ali's tone regained control as he spoke to his wife. "It's time you and the children move from the village and family compound to someplace else, at least temporarily . Your moving will assure the others they can remain there unharmed. My brothers are already hinting that the entire family is at risk on account of us. I want you to be safe."

"Where do you want us to go without you?" Shahgofta cried.

"I need to contact my cousin, Na'im. He has family in Karachi. But I can't reach him. Can you get his number for me?"

"You know I can't read numbers. Let me call Naser over."

When Shahgofta returned to the phone, Nur Ali, as always when this happened, chided her. "See? How many times have I told you to learn to read and write? You can't even read off a number to me!"

Shahgofta's illiteracy was perhaps a fault, but she made up for it with her brilliant skill in math, perfected by years of mental bookkeeping of household income and expenses, and of retaining a perfect mental record of gifts received for later reciprocation.

After calling his cousin Na'im and spending almost the entire night on the phone, conversations intermingled with customer interactions, Nur Ali's last call was back to Shahgofta, the third call that night, to inform her that his cousin, Na'im, would arrange her move to Karachi and get her and their two youngest children, Naseema and Naser, settled there with his relatives. She should begin packing up clothes and a few essentials. Na'im would help them relocate and get started with what they needed in a new apartment.

His wife had never left Swat and was horrified at the thought of what Karachi would bring. Visions of city scenes she had seen in movies froze her: hundreds of moving vehicles standing still and honking in traffic jams, thousands of human bodies packed tightly in streets and markets, moving in a single throng. The mere thought of traveling to get there represented an insurmountable threat.

"Will we come back here when this is all over?" Shahgofta asked, her voice shaking.

"Of course," the *qaida* comforted her as best he could. "We'll all come back together as a family. It's our home, after all." *How can we know what the future holds for us?* his eyes winced as he thought the unbearable.

Na'im was Nur Ali's most trusted cousin, on his mother's side, and the person through whom he sent most of his money home. Maternal cousins did not represent a potential threat as did paternal cousins and brothers when it came to disputes over family lands and inheritances. Maternal cousins made ideal marriage partners. The mistrust among paternal cousins was evident in the Pashto language, which distinguished friendly paternal cousin from hostile paternal cousin, or enemy. Na'im was the obvious choice for sending money home as well as entrusting his family with a major move.

And Karachi? Well, Karachi was a vast city teeming with Pashtuns and containing all the modern amenities one could dream of. Nur Ali heard about Karachi in the news almost daily, so he would know where his wife was, what was going on around her, and what to warn her about. He would be connected to her and partially informed via the media.

The night had been exhausting, but apart from dealing with a minor store situation, Nur Ali had solved two family issues: getting medical assistance to his granddaughter and taking initiative to move his wife and children to safety. In between all the calls home, he had also needed to call Bacha Gul twice for new phone card numbers and PINs, promising to send him money with Mir Zaman the next day.

7-ELEVEN

Being in an ethnic neighborhood and manned all night by one of their own, the 7-Eleven convenience store was a popular stop for the Pashtun cab drivers on night shift. One night, Mir Zaman came running into the store with Kashef. The two Swatis were driving their cabs on their night shift, talking as they did night after night on their phones to pass the time as they perused the city. A passenger had vomited in Kashef's cab, and Mir Zaman had suggested stopping in on Nur Ali, whose store may have a cleaning product. They burst into the store, and the three of them simultaneously spilled out a litany of warm greetings typical in Swat.

"Welcome."

"Don't be tired."

"May God spare you from poverty."

"May your house be blessed."

"Live in peace."

Nur Ali prepared tea for his guests: strong black tea with milk and much sugar, Pakistani style, borrowed from the British. They settled in a circle, squatting tightly behind the counter, and quickly rose each time someone entered the store.

As they each held their cup in both hands to warm themselves, Kashef began: "Nur Ali, the back seat of my car is drenched. I can't smell anything, and don't know if it's puke or piss. I swear, I think they do it on purpose when they see my name on the driver ID posted on my back seat, and they can't think of a more insulting thing to do. Do you have anything here to clean it up with?"

Mir Zaman interrupted him: "Hey, that's 'Mama' to you, young man, or at least 'Nur Mama.' Don't talk like you're not Pashtun anymore." Nur Ali was their elder and deserved due respect.

Nur Ali then also scolded Kashef on the same point. "And he," he motioned to Mir Zaman, "is Lala to you. Have some respect." "Lala" was the term Pashtuns used to address an older brother, or an unknown male peer, with deference. They all laughed, and the point was taken.

The cab drivers launched into their usual litany of complaints associated with the business, mostly regarding the vomiting and pissing in the back seat.

"I'm convinced it has to do with evil eye," suggested Mir Zaman. "I even had a talisman made to protect my cab, which I hang from the rearview mirror."

"Well," said Kashef, "the constant stink in my back seat is enough protection from evil. It's definitely undesirable to anyone."

"Be careful with evil eye," warned Nur Ali, who was a strong believer in the destruction that can be brought on by envy, or evil eye. "If someone compliments something you have, you want to make sure to give it to them, or give them something. And never eat food in public unless you're ready to share with everyone around you. You never know who is watching with hungry eyes. Don't let them envy something you have, or you'll attract trouble. Especially in this country, we have to be doubly careful and aware of evil because we don't always perceive it. It comes in different forms."

They all grunted and nodded in agreement. They were well aware of the rituals to chase out the evil eye, and they resorted to them when people fell prey to sudden maladies. Evil eye was believed to lie beneath most harms and catastrophes in one's personal life.

As the cab drivers had Nur Ali's ear, they shared with him the concerns that usually occupied their nightly discussions, being the expenses that nearly wiped out their income: car leases, parking woes and tickets, insurance, licensing fees, and the constant cleaning. They also shared stories of the hate talk they had to endure, the accusations of being "filthy Muslims" who were responsible for 9/11 and other terrorist attacks in the country. But the positives of the job had to do with their access to women.

"I had one in my back seat the other day," began Kashef, "who needed a ride to the airport. Thank God it was a long ride. I watched her in my rearview mirror while I drove. She applied her makeup, checked her phone, and looked out the window. We didn't make direct eye contact, but because she was so preoccupied, I was able to stare at her the entire way. Sometimes you get lucky like that."

"Sometimes," added Mir Zaman, "they engage in conversation, mostly when they've been drinking and are all giggly. It's fun to talk with them about silly things. We can't ever do that back home."

"Yeah," warned Nur Ali, "you're best off staying out of trouble. You can look and talk all you want, but you don't want to touch."

"You're just old," scoffed Kashef, remaining intent on knowing how to successfully approach American women.

"You know," interjected Mir Zaman, "all of us taxi drivers spend our driving hours on group calls, six or seven at a time, comparing stories of women we flirt with in our cabs, or women we see and desire as we peruse through the city streets on our night shifts."

"Yeah," Kashef was nodding enthusiastically. "We do that a lot. And you know about Niaz! He touches all he wants." Everyone had heard about Niaz, the young Baluchi who preyed on women alone at home when he made house calls as a cable service man, and then bragged about the ease of his conquests. Several among the exiles had girlfriends. Some were even married with the purpose of obtaining green cards, although these marriages almost inevitably turned sour and ended up in court or worse, with deportation.

A man walked in while they were talking, looking to buy a pack of cigarettes, and Mir Zaman, who spoke the best English, engaged in some light conversation with him. "Where you all from?" asked the man.

"Afghanistan," replied Mir Zaman. "We speak Pashto, our national language."

"Aren't they terrorists over there?" questioned the man, looking edgy and anxious to leave.

"Not everyone," said Mir Zaman. "Look at us. We're just trying to make a living here. We have families back home, just like you."

But the man still left without pursuing the conversation. And as soon as he left the store, the three of them began a heated discussion around the popular topic of identity. "I never say I'm Pakistani," began Mir Zaman.

"Sometimes," Kashef added in agreement, "I say I'm Indian." Sufficient experience with responses from Americans had made almost every Pakistani immigrant say the same thing. Urdu speakers tended to say they were Indian, while Pashto speakers also identified as Afghan. But since 9/11, ignorance and the media had turned the Pakistani into a terrorist, evoking fear and suspicion in the American psyche, and Pashtun pride did not extend far beyond their own closed circles.

Here among themselves, these three individuals from the same general area of Swat Pakistan, however, reveled in talking about their villages and memories of home. Kashef spoke about the hamlets close to his own near Topi, displaying an acute demographic as well as geographic knowledge. "In this hamlet, there are no public guest areas," he described. "In that hamlet, the houses are all concrete, the residents are wealthy and educated, and you won't see any turbans or pleated Afghan *burqas*."

Nur Ali gladly welcomed the opportunity to describe his village, Khwaza Khel, in detail. The hamlet sat on the main road alongside the Swat River going north to Madyan, Bahrain, and Kalam. South of Khwaza Khel in the lower foothills lay Mingora, which was the primary market town for Central and northern Swat. He assumed his listeners had visited Mingora, but neither had been even that far north. If a person wanted to travel north by bus from Peshawar, the capital of Pakistan's North-West Frontier Province in the valley, he would transfer in Mingora from the large bus to a smaller white van that continued winding along the Swat River to service villages north of Mingora to the farthest town, Kalam. There, Nur Ali added, the road ended in the high elevations of the Hindu Kush mountains.

"I've heard rumors," interrupted Mir Zaman, "that people up there are savage and live solely on potatoes, the only crop they can successfully grow. Any truth to that?"

"Absolutely!" replied Nur Ali with confidence. "And people in Kalam and beyond eat worms for meat." Feeling warmed that he had their attention, he pursued his description.

Traveling north from Mingora through the Malakand Pass and along the Swat River and Valley, hugged tightly on either side by steep mountains, you could see fields rising in tiered terraces to follow the steep grade. Clusters of homes were built the same way, like steps climbing the mountain. From the Peshawar Valley up the lush green Swat Valley to the northern mountains, you could see the structures change from mud in the valley, to stone and mud, and eventually to wood and stone in the far northern climes where forests abounded. Khwaza Khel lay halfway between Mingora and Kalam, and had nothing to attract anyone from farther than hamlets across the river or in the mountains who were seeking to market goods. If they needed items beyond the everyday, they traveled south to Mingora or north to Madyan.

Kashef and Mir Zaman, who had never traveled as far north as the popular tourist towns of Madyan and Bahrain, had heard about the treacherous bridges crossing the upper Swat River. Nur Ali, laughing, gave them a full report.

"There are no bridges to support vehicles," he started. "They're wooden slats suspended by ropes, and you always feel like you're going to fall through the slats. But the bridges rarely collapse. People cross with mules laden with bricks and cinder blocks to build homes on the other side. I've seen wedding processions run and dance across these swinging bridges! And north of Madyan is a cable hung between both sides of the river, from which hangs a sitting platform. A man can get himself to the other side by pulling the cable, or he can pull a woman across. I've never used that one," he added, enjoying the drama. His audience, entertained by the story, smiled and raised their eyebrows at each other.

"In my own village," Nur Ali continued, enjoying himself, and steering away from the bridges, "the paths leading away from the main road are all mud, and only a handful of people have concrete houses. You can always tell you're on the way to my house when your eyes begin to see above the mud and stone walls rising beside you, out to corn fields and more distant homes. There the valley opens up and you can look down onto the flat rooftops of the village below. You'll come be my guests one day when we all go home.

"Of course," he continued, "once you pass the houses and are in the open, the wind brings the smell of the buffalo slaughtering ground along the river. What a stench! Our women have to take that way to avoid the main path when they go into the village.

"And you won't hear any Urdu spoken in my area or see any women in the bazaar. We still stone women who are even suspected of illicit relationships. I saw a few stonings before I came here."

Kashef and Mir Zaman, who had only heard of these deaths by stoning in northern Swat, exchanged uncomfortable glances while motioning in Nur Ali's direction. Mir Zaman, preferring to change the subject to the time he'd done some touring around lower Swat, described the beautiful houses owned by the wealthy families in Mardan and Abotabad, large towns in southern Swat. He loved to talk about the kababs he had eaten at the renowned Abassin Restauran t sitting right over the water at Torbela Dam. And Nur Ali, who had once traveled north from Khwaza Khel to Bahrain, remembered a similar kabab house overlooking the raging Swat River.

Occasionally during their conversation, the phone rang, and Nur Ali assumed his managerial role. Shiriney called once to check that everything was good. Bacha Gul called to ask if his friend needed phone cards that night. Sherry called to have Nur Ali move the Altoids to the front of the display, and a man called to ask the store's location. But these calls were quickly dealt with and forgotten as the three returned to their needed escape.

Language was another inevitable topic of conversation when Pashtuns socialized, such as tonight, and Nur Ali had firm ideas on the subject.

"There are four essential languages you have to know," he counseled the others. "Pashto, Urdu, Arabic, and English. Pashto, because it is our native and family language. We speak it to show our Pashtun pride. Urdu, because it is our national language, the one we learn in school. Arabic, for Islam and for employment reasons. And English, because it is the common international language."

Mir Zaman and Kashef agreed, although in their southern areas of Swat, closer to Peshawar, they spoke more Urdu than he did in the north.

They loved to compare their own northern, hard dialect of Pashto, or Pukhto, to the southern soft dialects spoken by Wazir or Khattak Pashtuns, or that they had heard from Kandahari Afghans, and each one shared examples of "they say that; we say this."

Discussion of language inevitably led the friends to discuss poetry and popular music. Like most Pashtuns, they were familiar with the sung stories which filled buses, bazaars, tea and kabob houses throughout Pakistan and Afghanistan and Mir Zaman knew many musicians and their songs. Although Nur Ali was less knowledgeable about these, he had a special story to entertain his visitors.

"Once, we hosted the famous poet, Ali Heydar, from Mardan. His son and my brother Yusuf Ali had met in Qatar."

"No way!" exclaimed Mir Zaman. Ali Heydar was not a published literary poet, but was rather known for having written popular Pashtun legends in chapbook form, in simple verse which were then further popularized as they were sung and recorded by local known singers. "I love the tale of Yusuf Khan and Sher Banu." *

Nur Ali smiled and nodded, thinking of his own daughter-in-law who had been named after the popular story heroine.

"Isn't that the one where he marries a second wife he really loves when the first one can't have any children?" chimed in Kashef. "And the jealous first wife slanders her, alleging that she was flirting with a tobacco seller."

"Yeah," it was Mir Zaman's turn. "And when Yusuf Khan comes home to the scandal, he's left with no alternative than to slaughter her to save the

117

family's name and honor."

"It's sad, but very true of our culture," added Nur Ali.

"They made a movie of it," said Kashef. "I saw it in the cinema in Peshawar."

"Ali Heydar really came to your house?" Mir Zaman looked ready to jump up in excitement.

"I'm not kidding," continued Nur Ali. "His son and my brother had met in Qatar, and he came to visit us."

"No way!" exclaimed Mir Zaman.

"I'm not kidding," continued Nur Ali. "Ali Heydar. He brought a crate of mangoes for the house, and my brothers and I immediately set about killing a chicken while the women, who would only ever know their guest by the amount of food he ate and returned to them, started sifting and cooking rice and other delicacies that we ran up from the market for them. Everyone rushed around. Of course, the word spread fast, and other close friends and relatives were invited, which made our guest room look particularly small and crowded. One man spent the evening massaging Ali Heydar's legs. Another massaged the old poet's bald head. And when the music began, several guests tapped gently on empty clay water pots."

The thought of such a gathering inspired Kashef and Mir Zaman to begin reciting poetry from the homeland. Nur Ali was not so versed in classical poetry, but he entertained them with popular two-line verses he had learned from the cassettes played throughout bazaars and on buses.

"Spring has arrived, the trees have greened;

The trees of my soul beaten by hail ."

"Young girl, may your white-bearded father perish;

Sleeping by day, watching you by night."

"Men drink wine to intoxicate themselves;

But I am intoxicated by my friend's languishing eyes." **

Mir Zaman could not sing but had spent a portion of his youth memorizing poems from the famous classical literary poets, Rahman Baba and Khoshal Khan , who spoke of Pashtun pride and heroes and he, too, recited some verses. As for Kashef, he grabbed a can off the shelf and used the ring on his finger to tap a rhythm and create ambiance, as he might have on an earthen water pot. All three of these men found a way to temporarily shut out the foreign world they lived and struggled in and to immerse themselves in their home culture. For Nur Ali, it was a time to restore order and sense, even comfort, into his life of chaos. He hadn't scratched his arms all evening, and the pain in his back had subsided.

PAKISTAN BEFORE & NOW

As Nur Ali and his brothers had grown into adulthood, they decided to remain together in the family home, pooling resources and labor as an extended family. Their uncles separated off into their own homes, while their father, being the oldest of the siblings, held on to the ancestral home, to remain cared for by his sons' daughters-in-law. Each of the four brothers had a room, or home, for their family. And as the brothers' sons were married, they were also given their own room. Eventually, the younger three would move on, and Nur Ali, as the firstborn son, would keep the family home, according to tradition.

Nur Ali's parents had not lived to know the Taliban or the devastation of Swat. For them and others of their generation, and even for Nur Ali growing up, *talibs* were students, wards of the mosques and madrassas, or religious schools. The young boys were donated to these institutions by families for a variety of reasons. Sometimes they were orphans. Sometimes a family sacrificed their child to thank Allah for having spared the life of a previous child. It was a true sacrifice because the family would not see their son again, nor would he bring a daughter-in-law into the household. These *talibs* were housed and educated by the mosque, and trained to become religious preachers. Each night at dusk, the children roamed the streets and alleys of towns and villages with bowls, begging for food that they would take back to the mosque and share. Nur Ali's mother had always kept aside a small amount of whatever she cooked that night, to give the *talibs* when they came knocking. *Talib* was an honorable and praiseworthy title. Nur Ali often tried to explain to Matthew, his Christian coworker, the difference between good and bad Taliban in Pakistan

One night while on the phone with Bacha Gul, the two friends were on the topic of life and death when Nur Ali told him the story of his father's death.

"He died suddenly of a ruptured vein in his head. There was no treatment for it. We were eating lunch, and he suddenly groaned and asked for some peanuts. Sardar Ali went to hire a Suzuki, and we brought him to the doctor who then sent him to the emergency clinic in Mingora. He spent four days in the hospital. I gave blood to buy him a few days, but his time had come. He died, and here I am. He was a simple man who didn't understand the modern world."

"God forbid!" responded Bacha Gul. "When your time has come, it's God's will, and you have to accept it."

Death and dying occupied a special place for Pashtuns. Not only was it accepted calmly as God's will, it was recognized with ritual, with specific expectations for men and women. For both, however, narrating the story of a relative's death played a role in demonstrating their relationship to the deceased, and in displaying the proper genre and quantity of emotion. Enduring hardship and suffering was tantamount to being Pashtun.

Bacha Gul in turn told the story of his brother, who had died as a child in the village. "My brother was seven, pure and beautiful, and as fair as a foreigner. My parents took him to one doctor after another, and they all changed his medication, but the fever and vomiting never let up. My father was taking him to see a doctor in Peshawar, and in Mingora he had paid for a separate three-person seat on the bus for the two of them. The boy recited his final prayer three times and asked my father for a white scarf to tie his mouth closed.

When they reached the bus terminal, everyone climbed off, but the boy remained in the seat, eyes closed. My father frantically beat his head on the seats and benches, but the bus driver covered them both with a blanket and offered to take both father and son back to Madyan for three-hundred rupees. The bus stopped in our village, and the men in the bazaar helped my father carry my brother on a cot uphill to our compound.

Like a madwoman, my mother ran out without her veil, wailing, to meet the group along the path. Just the night before, my brother had described a weight on his chest. How could we know it was the weight of his own death?"

"God forbid! God forbid!" sighed Nur Ali, feeling the familiar dull pain in his back. "What a beautiful story." Void of emotion and self, the acceptance of and deference to God's will ruled without exception in Nur Ali's Pashtun psyche.

Nur Ali's memory took him to just after his father's death, when his mother had wanted to perform a pilgrimage to a holy shrine to pray for her deceased husband. Most Swatis could not afford the cost of travel to Mecca for that most illustrious pilgrimage, but they could budget a visit to Pir Baba, a renowned saint's shrine in Swat. Nur Ali took his mother on the small bus from Khwaza Khel to Mingora, where they transferred to a regular bus. He took care to always seat her by the window so that no one could rub against her or touch her in any manner. But it was a hot day, and while he as a man was permitted to walk around the busy bus depot and drink water and eat whatever was being sold, he felt badly for his mother who was obliged to remain aboard the hot bus, stifling under her burqa.

"Here, take this." He managed to bring her a tin cup of water, roasted corn and chopped sugar cane to suck on and spit out, which he handed to her through the window. Other younger women on the bus were breastfeeding sweat-soaked babies under their burqas, and the women onboard bonded quietly together, complaining about the heat and other discomforts of travel. But the bus would not leave until every seat was accounted for. When Bibi needed to relieve herself, Nur Ali had escorted her off the bus to a quiet street and told her to squat there, under the privacy of her own burqa. From there, it was another long bus ride to Pir Baba. He thought now that travel had not changed much back home.

They had reached the shrine toward evening, along with throngs of other people all pouring out from the buses arriving at the same time. Although they were together, they didn't speak, and Bibi walked behind her son. And while hundreds of people were moving toward the mosque and the shrine, a second wave of men was exiting the mosque, having just finished evening prayers.

Nur Ali recalled how he had led his mother along the lanes at the entrance, lined with venders selling rose petals, prayer beads, antimony, and scented oils. He had anticipated the throngs of beggars and had filled his pockets with coins to disperse. He then led her directly to the saint's tomb, which was surrounded and protected by a tall iron railing around which a thick crowd was slowly circling, stopping to weep and wail and hold the railings.

His mother had been horrified by the mass of people all squeezed in so closely, hands groping blindly to grab body parts. Finding a spot at the railing, she had stood there motionless reciting prayers and afraid to move on until she heard her son's voice and turned to see him motioning her to follow. He led her to a section where other women and children were sitting and lying on the floor, and then went to get her some bread and greens to eat for dinner, although he could not stay to eat with her in this area.

At several intervals throughout the night, Nur Ali came to get Bibi and lead her without a word around the tomb and pray, each time returning her to the women's area to rest. He knew his role of escort, that he could not allow her to be alone outside the protected women's space. He himself had spent the night awake either praying in the mosque or talking with other male escorts. They all seemed of the same opinion, that the shrine was a dangerous and aggressive place not made for women, but they simultaneously recognized that for their women the pilgrimage played a vital role , and going there was a non-negotiable demand that their men must abide. For the many people who would never travel to Mecca for the great pilgrimage, a visit to this local saint was second best. He was thrilled, however, when morning came, and it was time to head home again.

After his mother had fulfilled her last prayers to her deceased husband at Pir Baba, she remained in the compound several years, growing older and more senile, but not bothering anyone as they pursued their daily activities around her. Toward the end of her life, she took to wandering, and they had to tie her to her cot in the courtyard during the day, but the women kept her clean and freshly dressed. They combed through her hair for lice, and she was treated with dignity and respect as the family matriarch until she died.

Nur Ali had not been there to bury his mother as he had his father, although he did manage the funeral rites by phone with the mullah and spent two weeks inundated with phone calls bearing condolences. It was with his mother's death that Shahgofta had acquired the title of Bibi and become matriarch of the entire extended family. But now Nur Ali doubted his wife's strength in standing up to his brothers in his absence, so he doubled his efforts to maintain his authority over the home .

He was now in America. His brother, Yusuf, had migrated to Qatar for employment. While these two family breadwinners sent money home to keep the family coffers plentiful, Mahmad Ali and Sardar Ali remained home to look after the compound and farm the land, along with all the women and children. In addition, Mahmad Ali had started his own cement business, which did quite well with the growth of new construction in Swat, and people opting for concrete to replace the traditional mud and wood for homes. Sardar Ali had taken over their father's store in Khwaza Khel. He was planning to move his family into the village when Nur Ali returned to take over the family home.

As for the women, there were many benefits to remaining an extended unit. It took hours of tedious labor to keep a house going when there were no appliances, when water and power were limited, and many children needed care. The sisters-in-law each performed separate chores so a single person did not have to do it all. Although each woman provided a different part of the meals, they ate as a community. Just as food preparation was done on the ground sitting on low stools, dish washing was done sitting on the same stools, over a concrete slab in the courtyard to avoid the mud. The sisters worked together to pour water in slow even amounts from the metal pots lining the verandah, and to line the clean dishes on the cots in the sun to dry.

The younger unmarried girls went weekly to a special spot along the river or to the new laundromats in town to wash laundry, where they met up and gossiped with other girls from the village. And twice daily when the water came on, they all went out to the faucet to fill the household water pots. And when one of the women was ill, had just given birth, or could not carry her load for any reason, the rest were there to cover for her. Younger girls helped by caring for babies and toddlers.

Bread was the staple. Each day after lunch and each night after washing up from dinner, the women of the compound kneaded and prepared the dough for the next day. They were careful when cooking the bread to keep a small amount of raw dough to act as starter for the next day's batch. The dough sat overnight in a flat basket until the next day. The unleavened fried bread eaten during Rozha didn't need preparation, but the bread baked in the mud tandur had to rise. As soon as a girl was tall enough to lean over the tandur without difficulty, she was eligible to bake.

Of course, communal living also posed its difficulties for the ladies, who often quarreled over inequalities and the maintenance of seniority status and privilege.

One night Sabina complained to her brother-in-law at the 7-Eleven: "La-wangina received a package today from her husband in Qatar. Shoes, soap, and toys for her children."

"That's nice," responded Nur Ali, who never sent packages except through people traveling home.

"No, it's not," continued Sabina, slighted. "He sent nothing to me for my children. I have children, too, and life is hard for all of us living here together."

"Well," the *qaida* tried to placate his brother's wife, "I'm sure your husband gives you gifts on the sly also. Calm down. We must try and live together in harmony."

The system of sharing workload as well as everything else made it very difficult to maintain individualism or to possess anything on one's own. When Nur Ali began sending cell phones as gifts for his sons, soon every niece, nephew, son, and daughter were begging him for one. As head of family, Nur Ali was particularly made to feel the currents of jealousy and envy that ran rampant within the compound . Even his phone calls did not go unnoticed and were the target of envy and bickering. When he made his daily call to Shahgofta each day, he tried to exchange personal greetings with each of his sisters-in-law to ask about their lives and how they were managing.

During a nighttime call to keep each other company, Matthew once asked Nur Ali if he called home. "Are you kidding? I can call ten times a day, and you'd think I never called. My brothers ask why I don't call them. My sisters-in-law complain that I never call them. My sons and my daughters-in-law all say the same. I swear, I made twelve calls home last night. The more I call, the more they complain that I don't call."

7-ELEVEN

"Salam alaykum, Mama," it was Matthew's friendly voice checking in on Nur Ali as he did each night. "Anything new?"

"Just having trouble with the slurpy machine, which is leaking again tonight."

Matthew offered advice for a fix, and the conversation moved on.

"The police came to the store tonight, started Nur Ali. "They want to bring me in for questioning. I don't know what it's about."

"Be cautious," warned his friend. "Don't tell them anything more than what they ask. They're always looking for reasons to get rid of us. You applied for asylum, didn't you?"

Encouraged by acquaintances at the mosque who had convinced Nur Ali that his life here would be easier if he had asylum status, and armed with the belief that he could then go home for visits and still return for work, he had sought out a trusted lawyer in the community to initiate a request for asylum. But his decision was beginning to be clouded with doubts, and he thought he'd rather take his chances and return home to be with his family permanently. He was feeling the pain of growing old, of losing hope, of vainly holding the memory of feeling desired by his wife. He had to find ways to convince himself to continue, and the thought of going home provided that practical distraction .

In between dealings with customers, the two friends spoke lengthily that night, turning to the influence of Afghan refugees on their own lives back home.

"I know they are the same people as we are," said Nur Ali, "but you have to admit, they are really backward compared to us."

"You know," started Matthew, "I had a friend in the medical business, and I sometimes went with him to a village in the south where he brought supplies and talked with the local doctor. Once, an Afghan mujahed came in with an infected wound on his thigh. My friend asked what had happened and the Afghan said he had been shot during a battle in Afghanistan. The bullet had been removed, but the fighter suffered ongoing pain, and when he came over for a rest with his family, he treated himself for the pain in their traditional manner."

"Meaning what?" questioned Nur Ali.

"Well, he had wound some gauze real tight to make a kind of cork with it. Then he stood it up on his wound and set a coal to the tip, letting it burn slowly down so the heat intensified and burned him."

"Allah!" cried Nur Ali in disbelief. "Was he trying to replace one kind of pain with another?"

"I guess so. He said he did it frequently. But the gauze must have been dirty this time and he got infected," offered Matthew in explanation.

"Those Afghans live on the floor, not like us on cots and stools," Nur

Ali began his usual diatribe against the group. "They let their animals shit all over. I heard their houses are always filthy. They burn fires inside and blacken the walls. They always smell of smoke." And as he spoke these words, he immediately regretted them. He inhaled deeply and felt the pang as he recalled the lingering smell of wood smoke that clung to his own wife's clothes when they lay together. *But,* he justified his thoughts, *we never burned our fires inside the house, but out in the courtyard.*

"Still," added Matthew, "what choice did they have, living in those camps? I'm glad they've gone home. Everyone belongs in their own country."

Matthew, who had suffered persecution as a Christian in Pakistan, had immigrated to a Christian country, and now endured the same ethnic hate as a Pakistani in America. He often expressed that he didn't have a home where he felt free and comfortable. But he trusted Nur Ali, and the two passed many hours together in such conversation while at their separate work places.

PAKISTAN NOW

"Salam alaykum."

"Walaykum salam. How are you?" replied Shahgofta.

"Not well. My head is spinning from always listening to this foreign language. My back and hips hurt from standing here night after night. And if my back breaks, I won't be any good to you or anyone else, will I?" In the same breath, he shifted gears. "How are things with you and the children? How is Sher Banu handling her pregnancy? Have you heard from the boys? From the village?"

"Everyone is fine, thank God," she replied.

Satisfied that her tone matched her words, he pursued. "Now tell me about your trip," urged Nur Ali. He had not spoken to his wife during the past four days while she was traveling to Karachi.

"It was long and strenuous beyond words. It was a nightmare," she began. "First we sat on a bus from Khwaza Khel to Mardan, with three of us squished on a two-person bench. Naseema was by the window, and me in the middle, with Naser on the aisle. Poor thing had to hold on to the seat in front of us to keep himself from falling off."

"What a good boy, to look after you that way. You've raised him well. You were protected, weren't you?"

"Yes," she continued, "but so squeezed in there, with our bundles on our laps. Naser managed to load our bigger bundles with bedding and some pots and pans on top of the bus, but we carried our clothing with us. Fortunately, we didn't have any babies, but I knew that Naser would have preferred a seat to himself rather than having to sit one cheek on, one cheek off the bench for the sake of propriety. Even Naseema whispered at one point that she wished she could sit up on the roof with the men, and we all laughed at her. All the way to Peshawar it was awful."

"Well," Nur Ali tried to make her see the bright side, "at least God kept you safe. Did Na'im see to your needs?" His practical side kept him from sympathizing with her discomfort.

"Of course. At every stop he and Naser brought us water and something to eat. And Naser escorted Naseema and me to quiet spots where we could pee under our burqas."

"Did you get on a bigger bus from Peshawar, and was it any better?" asked Nur Ali, hoping for better news.

"Somewhat. From then on, Naseema and I sat in the back of the bus with other women, where we were still smashed together, but not as badly. When the bus stopped we ladies would get off together and walk to an isolated field or other area for our toilet needs. One woman told me she had previously done the trip by train, stuffed in a compartment with only women and children all sitting almost on top of each other. She said when the train pulled into a station, it was so crowded that men would push the women and children in through the windows to make sure they got on. They couldn't even move to use the toilet! It sounded foul."

"I've heard about those trains," agreed her husband.

"But listen to this. Another Pashto-speaker riding with us worked as a customs official. She had a job stopping vehicles at certain checkpoints, and she made two hundred thousand rupees during her time there. She just took money from people, overcharging and keeping the excess for herself. She said everyone did it, and it made for a terrific source of income for her family."

"God forbid!" Nur Ali was horrified both by the corruption and by the fact that it was a woman.

"Most of the women on the bus spoke Urdu, though, so we couldn't talk too much with them. And Naser sat with Na'im."

"You'll have to learn some Urdu," Nur Ali teased his wife, who could not speak the national language beyond a few stock phrases she had learned in school . Naseema had learned more but had never spoken it. In their village, Urdu was only spoken by men and in the bazaars, never at home or by women. "Tell me more," he urged her to report all the details. Tonight it was Shahgofta's turn to talk. Nur Ali rubbed his lower back and enjoyed hearing her talk, even though the details of her story did little to comfort him.

"It took us three days and two nights for the entire journey. The bus occasionally stopped for the men to get off and pray, and whenever there was an accident, it stopped so they could get off and look at the wreck. Each night, the bus stopped at a bus depot, and the four of us stayed in a room that opened to the parking lot where the buses were parked. That was twenty rupees for each night. The damp mud floor in one of them was covered with orange peels and mutton bones from other people. And you should have seen the flies…a cloud of them!"

"Traveling is not easy in our country. You were lucky you weren't alone. Can you imagine what it must be like for a woman traveling alone?" The *qaida* felt a tinge of pride for his wife and her experiencing the real world, but this feeling was also shadowed by another of remorse that he had not been the person there to protect his family and see to their needs.

"I feel sorry for any woman who has to be alone," agreed Shahgofta. She continued her story. "The guys went to pray and eat with other men in the tea and kabab shops, while we had to stay cooped up in a tiny fly-infested room. At least we had a toilet. Naser brought us dinner: some bread and lentil stew, along with yogurt and radishes—and a great pot of tea. It was nice to stretch out and lie down after the long days of sitting.

"When we got to Karachi on the third day," pursued Shahgofta, "I could just sit speechless and watch all the bustle. I've never seen so many people or so much commotion. Na'im and Naser gathered our packages, and we took two rickshaws to his family's apartment building. I'd never seen rickshaws. You know what I'm talking about? They're tiny. Naseema and I sat in one with our bundles, and Naser rode in another one with Na'im. I was petrified we'd get separated and lost. I didn't know where we were going. But our driver followed theirs, and we finally got to Na'im's family's apartment."

"Did they welcome you nicely?"

"Oh, yes. They certainly did. The moment we arrived, they brought tea and massaged our legs and showed us the bathroom. We were able to wash and do our prayers. And they prepared a fabulous meal with chicken, rice, and okra. It was a treat. Tomorrow they are helping us look for and move into an apartment in the same building. We'll have a phone, and I can call you regularly."

"How are the kids?"

"They're tired, like me, but they're okay," responded Shahgofta. "They're young, and will handle this more easily. Then she added, "I miss our mountains and the open fresh air."

"You'll get used to it," Nur Ali tried to encourage her. But he knew the change of environment would be as challenging for Shahgofta as it had been for him. "I wish I were there with you," he added. He closed his eyes and tried to see his wife's face as he had last seen it. As for his children, he could not imagine them at all. He longed to hold them all. He felt the familiar knot of fear in his stomach, and slowly scratched his arm, but tried to convince himself he had done the right thing in relocating his family. For now, they were safe.

7-ELEVEN

One evening before Michael's shift ended, Mo stopped by to chat, and their conversation moved to the topic of dreams. Nur Ali, who was a big believer in the message of dreams, told them about the nightmare in which he woke up without his beard.

"That's a big worry for you. Your beard means the world to you," conceded Mo. "My worst nightmare is when I wake up and feel like there is something in the room, but I'm too scared to get up and confront it. So I just lie there."

"I've had that, too," chimed in Michael. "Only in my dream, the thing—sometimes a gruesome looking hag of a woman—gets closer and closer, till I feel suffocated."

"Yes, I've had the same thing," added Nur Ali. "Occasionally, it feels like a great weight climbs onto me and sits on my chest. I've had the same nightmare several times since being here. Several people at the mosque have talked about the same thing. One man bought himself a talisman to protect himself. He thought he was being possessed by spirits."

"It's really bad," agreed Michael. "Someone told me it was because of the way I sleep, and that I should take care to sleep on my side and never on my back."

"I don't know," said Mo. "It's some of the crazy stuff that happens to us in this country ."

The three friends took some comfort in knowing they had a shared experience, unaware that the nightmare was the same that plagued so many refugees and immigrants, and resulted from the excessive stress they faced on an ongoing basis.

PAKISTAN NOW

Nur Ali experienced his wife's transition vicariously as he listened to her accounts on the phone. For Shahgofta, who had spent her entire forty-seven years of life life in an extended family community in the village, the move to Karachi was a cruel change of circumstance at first. Na'im was able, after a week of lodging her with his relatives, to find a small apartment in the same building for her and the two children. But for a woman who rarely, if ever, left the house, this meant social isolation for her, and also landed a huge workload for her to handle on her own.

The aging exile knew very well that when a man left the extended unit to establish his family as a nuclear one, it was his wife who tended to bear the brunt of it. Naser was still only fifteen, and was quickly placed in school, with Na'im's help. Naseema remained home with her mother, though she was pursuing her schooling at home via a correspondence course. But their older daughters-in-law, Rabia and Sher Banu, had remained in the village compound with their aunts, Nur Ali's sisters-in-law.

Taking in new daughters-in-law traditionally entailed an additional work force for an aging Pashtun matriarch, and allowed her to relax a little more. But Shahgofta had been stripped of her privileges and hurled into a situation where she had to assume all the household responsibilities, and the children; it was taking its toll on her. The *qaida* could see all this but felt helpless in each of their conversations. The itching in his arms intensified.

"It's all so different," she complained to him. "I can still scrub the laundry in a large flat tub on the floor, but there is no tandur to bake the bread. Na'im's sister had to show me how to use the electric coil to heat a cast iron pan for cooking it. And it's taking me time to get used to doing everything differently and get it right. I keep burning the bread. All my cooking methods need readjusting on the electric burners." Her voice was raised and trembling, and he could tell that she was on the verge of tears.

"Don't worry," he tried his best to calm her agitation. "You'll be perfect at it by the time I get home."

"And I miss the sun and our open courtyard," Shahgofta continued, almost as if she hadn't heard him. "I can see it shining outside through the window, but I don't dare go out in the streets. Naseema has gone out walking with the girls from Na'im's house and says there is a garden not too far, but I don't have the courage to venture out yet."

When Naseema got on the phone with her father, he asked what she was cooking for dinner that day. "Bread and tea," she told him.

He immediately heard the faint hesitation in her voice. His daughter had not intended to reveal their lack of food. "What?! You need potatoes, lentils, and some meat."

"Not today, *Qaidada*." Her quiet voice echoed with complacency.

"Put your mother on the phone," he commanded Naseema. And when Shahgofta was listening, he told her, "You need to get some meat. I don't want my kids thinking that I don't provide for them. You can get some ground beef for thirty rupees."

The *qaida* was feeling at a loss, and although Shahgofta never uttered a word of complaint about her situation, the urgency to get an older male to watch over them was upon him .

This can't go on! I have to fix it.

By the end of that week, he had arranged for their oldest son, Ahmad, to come live with his mother in Karachi, along with his wife, Rabia, and their three children. This provided companionship and assistance to Shahgofta, as well as an adult male to look after the women and make decisions. Ahmad and Rabia would move into the one bedroom with their children, while Shahgofta and her children would occupy the main room.

From a world away behind his 7-Eleven counter, once again the exiled head of family had resolved a major family crisis and maintained the balance of forces within the clan. Against all he had ever wished for and believed in, however, this extraction of his wife and now his oldest son to Karachi marked the first step in Nur Ali's transition from the extended family unit he had always known, into a nuclear one. He pushed on his lower back, but the pressure did not seem help lighten the pain.

He called her a third time later that same night. "Do you have honey in the house?" Nur Ali asked Shahgofta. "How much does honey cost these days?" He paused. "Never mind the cost. Send Naser to get some." Nur Ali knew honey was a special food in Islam, and Swat was celebrated throughout Pakistan for its honey production. He liked to know there was a small amount in the house at all times—like a talisman of protection—and often asked about it.

One night soon after having conducted the new arrangement, when Nur Ali called, he found his wife in a frenzy.

"My daughter-in-law and I quarrel all the time. She's been stealing from the household stock for her children, accused Shahgofta.

"Let me talk to her," the *qaida* assumed his role as mediator in an attempt to calm the sparks.

When Rabia got on the phone, however, her own accusations flew: "Bibi favors her younger children over her older son and his children. And she is having me take on all the house work."

"Put Bibi back on," requested the *qaida*, debating in his mind how he would resolve this. It was always a matter of food supplies, household goods, chores, or money.

"The girl shows no sympathy toward my ailments and fatigue," Shahgofta sobbed, "and she never asks how I am feeling. I am her elder, after all."

The *qaida*'s helplessness deepened. "Can't you find some way to get along?"

But by now Shahgofta was on a roll: "She is trying to sour our son against his parents."

The *qaida* had to intervene, as always via the phone, in this and many similar disputes. As he wondered at how different this was than in his father's time, he persisted and admonished Rabia through the receiver. "You are our daughter-in-law. You must respect, and look after your mother-in-law, and you must also take on more of her workload."

Then he chided his son, Ahmad: "You need to keep your wife in line."

He addressed them each in turn from his 7-Eleven counter, as they passed the phone around the room and listened without answering back. He reminded them each that they needed to live together in harmony, that the move caused them all to readjust, to realign their roles, and that they needed to be patient until they settled into a routine.

Although the *qaida* did all this, he knew his words fell on deaf ears and that without his presence, the fighting would persist.

The knot of anxiety ate away at his stomach and it felt to him like an apple corer emptying him out.

7-ELEVEN

The 7-Eleven was the target of so many robberies that Nur Ali had lost count. Momen Khan and Shiriney suggested the mounting number might be ethnic hate crimes executed by other minorities vying for resources or directly targeting their local neighborhood of obvious Muslim and Indian flavor. Since 9/11, Mulsim-owned stores had had their windows broken and experienced violence and robberies. The incidents at the 7-Eleven happened especially during the night shift. Periodically, the police would stop in on their round, but more frequently, they responded to calls after the fact. Nonetheless, Nur Ali used the threat of police in attempts to deter potential situations. Once he had noticed a man with a knife standing in front of the drinks cooler and told him, "The cops is coming; if they see your knife, they arrest you. Take your knife and go." He took it all in stride and never lost his nerve.

In all his years of managing the night shift, he had never been seriously injured. Night assaults were strictly for the cash register, and Nur Ali never resisted or attempted any heroics. The greatest challenge came not during, but after the assault. After ascertaining no one had been hurt, and getting over the trauma of the injury if one was involved, came delivering the report to the police and to 7-Eleven Headquarters. Nur Ali always remained calm, conscientious, and methodical during his report delivery. He knew the routine, even if he didn't understand each question being asked, and he knew that after calling the police to come, he had to call and make an official report and request a case number.

After fifteen years in the US, Nur Ali still could not speak English well, and required an interpreter for any official communication. He recited his narrative numerous times to authorities, superiors, colleagues, friends, and to family members. The police tended to appreciate his calm demeanor, though they raised an eyebrow and mused over his matter-of-fact description of thieves as innocent victims of need. They perceived him as a naïve, simple immigrant, too stupid to cause any harm. He never mentioned violence or threat, even on occasions where a thief had held a gun to his head. Nur Ali considered himself removed from anything in America or in his workplace; if it did not concern his family or situation at home, it was of no real consequence to him. Nonetheless, neither the questions nor the answers were always fully understood, and much went unreported.

One particular night, the store had been robbed twice by the same perpetrator. Sherry had already filed a report after the first incident in the afternoon. The police were just finishing up and leaving when Nur Ali arrived for his seven o'clock shift. Then, after midnight, when he was alone in the store, he had to call to report the second incident.

"Hello, 9-1-1," began the responder.

"Yes, sir…my store is rob. Please give me the case number," began Nur Ali, getting right to the point.

"What happened?"

"My store is rob."

"Okay, you had a robbery?" pursued the 9-1-1 operator.

"Yeah."

"Okay, is everyone okay?"

"Yeah, I'm okay, sir."

"Was anyone injured?"

"No injured."

"First and last name."

"My name is Nur Ali."

"Can you give me details?"

"The guy come five o'clock too. The same guy."

"What time?"

"I don't know the time. Maybe you tell me…half hour before. Because I have no register. I no take out the receipt. Yeah." Nur Ali was trying to explain that the robbery had occurred twice, a first time at five in the afternoon and a second time a half hour before he called 9-1-1, but because the register had been removed with the first robbery, he could not check the receipt for the exact time the second robbery happened.

"Are you the only employee working?"

"Yes, sir," continued Nur Ali.

"Did you call the store manager?"

"No, I no call, because these people is sleep now." The loyal employee was too respectful of Momen Khan and Shiriney to wake them in the middle of the night.

"And did you call the field consultant?"

"I call, yeah. He is coming here."

"Your field consultant?"

"I don't know. A lot of cops here in the store." The employee was referring to the afternoon incident.

"What kind of weapon did the guy have?" The 9-1-1 operator was trained to move on rather than pursue a misunderstood topic.

"He no weapon. Nothing."

"No? What did he take?"

"He no say to me nothing. But he bring the coffee."

"He what?"

"He bring the coffee. Coffee. Coffee. He put on the counter. I say, "One, thirty-five." If I open register, he took the register." Nur Ali was getting impatient with the operator's inability to understand the simple facts of the crime as he was reporting them.

"Okay, so you opened the register and what happened?"

"If I open register… he is very tall, big guy. He took the register, and he run away. We have no register right now. One register he took at five o'clock. The other he took right now."

"Can you give me a description of the suspect?"

"232 Crimson Boulevard," Nur Ali offered the store address.

"Right, but can you give me a description of the suspect?"

"Scription number?"

"Description, like what he looked like."

"I don't know, sir, about this."

"I'm sorry?" It was the operator's turn to get frustrated. His questions were all being met with dead ends.

"Description number?"

"Yeah, do you know...was he a black male, or..." Maybe different wording would yield better results.

"Oh! Yeah, he's, he's white man, sir."

"Okay, white male?"

"Yeah, he's white man. He rob the store five o'clock the daytime. And he come again. Yeah, but we have no register right now."

"Okay, about how old would you say he is?"

"Thirty-five."

"And how tall?"

"Yeah, very heavy guy."

"Heavy?"

"Heavy. Very heavy, very strong."

"Okay. About six feet tall? Or less?"

"More than six. Maybe six hundred fifty and more."

"Probably 200 pounds?"

Yeah. Maybe more. He's so big."

"And did he have any weapons?"

"No weapon. He no weapon."

"Was he in a car, or was he walking?"

"Yeah, he walking. Yeah, he go number third block. I run away with him. He go number third block."

"Okay, he left walking, then? He just came in, took the register, and left?"

"No, he bring the coffee cup."

"Okay, and do you know how much money was in the cash register?"

"I don't know, sir. He took all register."

"He just robbed the register and left the store?"

"Yeah, he left the store, yeah."

"Did you call your field consultant?"

"Yeah, I called. I called the cops. They're coming. He took the report. He asked me about everything. After, he go now. He look the video."

"Were you scared?"

"I never scared! Why I scared?!" Nur Ali's sense of practicality allowed only action, not emotion.

"No, I mean, you did not feel threatened?"

"No, I am alright. I'm never scared from these people."

"I understand, but did you feel threatened when he took the register?"

"He took the register. He so strong. Me and he fight, but he took the register."

"Okay, so you tried to fight him, and he took the register?"

"Yeah, the cash drawers. Not register, but cash drawers, he took."

"Okay, did he hit you, or anything like that?"

"No, he not hit me. He just need the money." Nur Ali almost sounded sympathetic toward the thief.

"Did he tell you anything?"

"He no speak me nothing. He jump. He jump and took the register. Yeah."

And so, as so many times before and after, Nur Ali tried to dutifully report the crime. It was a frustrating experience on both ends, but he had accomplished what was needed. His bosses would be satisfied. Only on these occasions, or in dealing with store cashiers when shopping did he ever speak English beyond the memorized lines he used at the cash register with customers.

Both in testifying to the robberies, and to Shahgofta, Nur Ali's response to the crimes remained matter-of-fact: "There is no law or order here. They break in, and they steal stuff." This was like any other time, and robberies happened practically every week. They elicited no emotion from Nur Ali; he accepted them as a part of life here. They were of no consequence unless they challenged his core beliefs. His upbringing in Swat to be clan leader and show no emotion served him well here.

Two things aroused Nur Ali's ire. One was the desecration of home privacy by uninvited males, and the other was a crime for which Nur Ali had no tolerance—stealing from the poor. The 7-Eleven had a policy of keeping a bowl full of change on the counter, a donation box for use by the poor and homeless. As a Muslim instilled with a duty to look after the poor and to provide food for the entire community on certain occasions, he was particularly incensed when anyone stole from the donation box.

He recounted each occurrence of this for days following the incident, to everyone who listened on the other end of his phone. He recalled and recited for them once again his father's teaching to him about the purpose of fasting: "It is to learn the hunger of the poor, and then be more sympathetic toward them! The pain we suffer in our stomachs is to teach us the dull pain that the ill live with. So long as you have not suffered these pains, you will never understand mankind, and you will walk through life proud and untouched, never going anywhere." These lessons permeated his being, were relearned each year during Ramadan, and were echoed viscerally each time they were violated. Repeating them aloud helped him regain a sense of order.

On the one hand, he showed generosity toward people in need, as with the use of the store phone, toilet, or the lack of a total payment. If a customer was short of money to pay for a purchase, Nur Ali took it from the donation box and told them it was okay.

On the other hand, he had no tolerance for the substance abuse he judged in the homeless, drunks, or drug users who sullied the store on his shift. Often, in the midst of conversation with Shahgofta, he described his disgust of these individuals: "These sons of dogs come in here looking for handouts. They show no pride or modesty in the way they dress. They're crazy drunk. They lose their minds and piss their pants."

What Nur Ali saw and experienced during his shift is what fed his understanding of Americans and his description of them to folks back home. According to what he witnessed from his store in its poor inner-city neighborhood, Americans in the twenty-first century were indigent and jobless, reduced to stealing or begging in the streets. This was definitely not a place he would recommend that anyone from his family come to find viable employment. And he certainly saw nothing in this society that made him want his daughters there. He felt hated by Americans, and he hated back. There would be no breaking of these barriers. But he neither consciously wished nor inflicted harm on anyone. He just knew he had no desire or tolerance to be one with them, so he kept his focus on returning home.

In his calls to family after the robbery that night, Nur Ali neglected to even mention the robbery, as though it had not occurred. Not that he intentionally avoided the subject or tried to protect his family from worrying about him, but he did not consider the robbery of any consequence relative to what was happening at home or to his task of resolving family issues.

PAKISTAN NOW

Loyal to the entire family, the *qaida* continued his calls not only to Shahgofta in Karachi, but also to the village compound, which was still his by law, and where Sher Banu remained. Sabina and Lawangina reported that it had been raining for two days, and everyone was getting tired of being closed up in their dark rooms without access to the muddy courtyard. They managed to cook on the concrete verandah over smoky fires from damp wood.

With the rains, mud became a topic of conversation.

"Our courtyard is a bed of mud," complained Sabina.

Nur Ali was from a village where, although concrete had begun to replace wood and stone in construction, and a major highway had been build to connect the bazaar in Swat to the capital in Islamabad, there had been no concrete paving in the village when he was last there. With any excessive rain, the dirt paths in the mountains became mudslides, as did the courtyards in all their home compounds.

"I know," sympathized the *qaida*. "I remember. In America there is no soil, and no matter how much it rains here, it generates no mud." This fact, as he experienced it from his inner city 7-Eleven, fascinated him.

"Sher Banu has more flour than she needs," started Sabina again, "but the roof of her room is leaking, and she can't keep it dry. Why don't you tell her to let us hold onto it for her."

The rain and confinement resulted in increased edginess and quarreling among the women, and the *qaida*, blind to visual cues, heard it plainly in the emotion behind their elevated pitches. This was clearly an attempt to deprive Sher Banu of her food supply, and he could not help but assume the blame: *I've left my youngest daughter-in-law, the last member of my nuclear family, alone and pregnant to fend for herself in the compound with her elder inlaws who have no particular affection for her, and who now want to take her source of bread.*

By the same token, she was his favorite niece, and he attempted to speak with her daily, and to make sure she always received a portion of the money he sent home, to spend on herself and her daughter Nazia. In order not to offend his own son, however, he reminded his daughter-in-law not to tell her husband about the extra spending money. In tears today, she pleaded with her father-in-law for permission to stay a while at her parents' house.

"You need to ask your husband for that authority," he replied. "But until he grants it, you need to do whatever you can to get along with your aunts and everyone in the compound. They are your elders, and you must respect them and not argue with them. Have patience. It is what Allah teaches us to do in hard times. Just keep to yourself, do your chores, and tend to your daughter. I'll send you some money to get her bangles."

Once again, unable to share other than a few moments of words with the girl, the *qaida* resorted to lecturing, his default mode of communication.

After he hung up, however, Nur Ali fretted over Sher Banu. With the knot in his stomach ever tightening, he tried all the more desperately to hold on to order, to make things right and felt obligated, as always, to mediate and find solutions to the quarreling. He called Shahgofta and riled about Iqbal's neglect of his own wife. He called his brothers in the village, beseeching them to reason with their wives to get along with Sher Banu. He contemplated finding her a separate arrangement, and finally gave his consent as *qaida* to send her back to her parents' house temporarily. He had to accept the obvious. Since when, especially in hard times, would a young mother find favor with her paternal uncles' wives? In his son's absence, he just had to wait for an opportune moment to move her.

"Thank you, *Qaidada*," responded Sher Banu meekly. He could hear her despair.

With his brothers and his son, Iqbal, still in hiding, Nur Ali, as *qaida*, supported not only his wife and children in Karachi now, but all the women and children remaining in his compound . He sent money orders every two weeks to his cousin Na'im in the village, who signed for them and delivered the cash to Sabina, Nur Ali's oldest sister-in-law. The *qaida* then instructed her on to how distribute the money for his home's expenses, as well as to individuals for their personal needs. Most importantly, Sabina was to accumulate cash for his return. For the exiled worker, it was the closest thing to a retirement account. But from his distance, Nur Ali could not monitor how his money was actually being distributed. Was Sher Banu getting her share? Was his own retirement savings being put aside? A woman like Sabina would be more loyal to her own husband's demands than to a distant brother-in-law. But what other choice did he have? Adding to his paranoia, Nur Ali was also growing suspicious of his brother Mahmad Ali's motives.

Any hostility between the brothers could endanger his savings.

From his 7-Eleven counter in the wee hours of the morning, eyes staring blankly at the colorful round metal tins of tobacco, the *qaida* continually reminded them all that they needed to live together, cook together, work together as one home, look after each other, and use the money for the kids and household expenses.

"What point is there to my being and working here," he repeatedly cried to Shahgofta, if I can't provide for my family?"

7-ELEVEN

Besides keeping order in his own home back in Pakistan, Nur Ali was reputed in the local immigrant community for networking to help new arrivals get situated with housing and jobs. Particularly if they were expatriate Swat Pashtuns, he was there for them, vouching for them, referring them as a cousin, doing whatever it took to get them started.

Tonight, Bacha Gul called and announced the arrival of a father and son from Swat, both of whom needed work. Nur Ali knew of a group house in town where the two could share a room. He spoke directly with the son, whom Bacha Gul put on the phone.

"I know a house close by," he addressed the young man, "where someone just left and they have a spare room. I'll let them know you're coming. As for work, I know your father is an elder. You won't be offended if I get him work cleaning and taking out the trash?"

"Of course not, Kaka," replied the young man. "We're grateful for anything you can find for us. Our journey to get here was a long one."

"As for you, don't you worry about a thing, continued the exile, confident with his abilities. "We'll fix you up with something. Jobs are scarce these days. You may get twenty hours here and ten hours there. But we'll hook you up with something. You'll be okay. You're one of us, and we take care of each other."

Nur Ali then brainstormed with Bacha Gul. "Isn't there a family from Konja with a fried chicken place? And how about Mir Zaman: is he looking for a partner to share his taxi with him? Do you think Rahim Jan could get him set up with a food cart? We have to find work for our Swat people."

"The problem with the food cart," responded Bacha Gul "is that he needs a driver's license and a permit. It takes time. And the income isn't good relative to overhead expenses. It costs seven hundred dollars a month to rent the cart and another five hundred and fifty per month for garage space. And what would he use as a tow vehicle? That's not something you can do overnight. The carts are usually owned by a single family, so Rahim Jan doesn't need to hire from outside. Plus, if you listen to the food cart folks, they'll warn you that the investment and overhead aren't worth the income."

Undeterred, Nur Ali hung up and immediately resorted to calling Momen Khan. "Do you need anyone?" he began. "I've got a guy here, a good reliable worker, has all his teeth." Nur Ali's recommendations of fellow Pashtuns for work reflected the qualities looked for back home. "He's strong and not afraid of hard work. I can vouch for him in every way. His father can also do cleaning and easy stuff. They're honest and won't eat store food or steal from you. Do you have anything for either of them? I'll train them here with me for no pay."

Nur Ali was able, following a flurry of calls, to get some night hours at another 7-Eleven for the young man. Proud of his accomplishment, he called the man and told him, "It's beautiful, easy work. 7-Eleven is a great opportunity in America. You get paid cash, six dollars an hour to start, but

I'll try to get you bumped up to seven an hour. That's decent money for us. And there's no boss watching over you."

"That's terrific," cried the young man, who was prepared to start immediately.

"But," warned the experienced exile, "night work also involves danger, not like the easy day work. There is the risk of shooting, death, stealing, insults, and lots of other trouble. Can you handle it? People come in running from trouble and need to hide or use the phone for help. You need to call 9-1-1 when they come in shot up and bleeding. You need to report incidents to the police."

"I can do anything," announced the young man, full of confidence.

"And you don't work just with Muslims," Nur Ali added for good measure. "Christians work here too. They're good people."

"This is America," concurred the new exile. "Everyone works together here."

Nur Ali had such a wide reputation for job brokering that even non-Pashtuns sought out his assistance to find openings in the community, and he always reassured them and promised to find them something somewhere.

PAKISTAN NOW

"Salam alaykum," began Nur Ali when he heard the receiver pick up his call.

"Walaykum salam," responded Shahgofta, her voice suggesting that she had been interrupted.

"How are you?" he was not deterred by her indignant tone. "How is the situation? Have you spoken to the family? I think of our daughter-in-law every day, close to giving birth and alienated from us. I was absent at my son's wedding, at his first child's birth, and now we will all be away from her for this birth."

"They say it's still bad," she reported. "Soldiers all over. The rain is causing mudslides and flooding, ruining homes and crop terraces. They sent out an evacuation notice, warning people to get out."

Every phone call to Pakistan opened with a question as to the situation, and whether it would be safe for Nur Ali to come home. Now the weather was adding to the political and legal stress. After fifteen years, he was beginning to experience physical pain and exhaustion. He was slowing down. He dreamed of returning to the green mountains of Swat, or even to Karachi, if it meant being with family again. But everyone had a different scenario to paint for him, tainted by personal motive. Those who relied on the money he sent them indicated a grim situation, certainly too dangerous for his return, while those who had nothing to gain or lose, or didn't know the extent to which they subsisted on his earnings, claimed the situation was peaceful and propitious. The *qaida* was confused and did not know whom to believe. And now the flood meant more woes, more losses, more reasons for *him* to remain in America and send funds to help out.

Even his oldest son Ahmad, now in Karachi with his mother, responded to Nur Ali's complaints of bad health by saying, "Take care of yourself, *Qaidada*. You'll be no use to anyone if you get sick."

At a lull in their conversation, Shahgofta, who had stopped her prayer to answer the phone, asked, "Have you done your prayers?"

"It's four o'clock in the morning! Since when does anyone pray that early? How many sections of prayer have you done?"

"Two. I still have more to go," she replied.

Undaunted, he began telling his story for the day. "I went to court for my hearing today, to see if they'll grant me political asylum. They held a Bible in front of me and told me to put my hand on it and swear to God."

"And did you?"

"Are you mad? Allah would know if I swore to another god but Him. He does not forgive this sort of thing. It would be sacrilege and make me a *kafer*, an infidel! Of course, I didn't. They told me to go home, and that my case was dismissed until I would swear on their Bible. Now they will kick me out."

In his heart, Nur Ali had some time ago abandoned the idea of remaining in America, but his request for asylum, claiming death threats back home, had allowed him to remain and work here all these years. Now that he was feeling ready to return home, he did not believe he had to submit to court demands. On the contrary, he felt empowered to stand up to these.

"But what do other Muslims do?" asked Shahgofta.

"They are hypocritical bastards. They live one thing and say another. They are all infidels!" His father's warnings about the evil of hypocrisy were his most deeply engrained lessons, a strong thread to a more stable past.

On a roll, Nur Ali told his wife a story he had heard recently in a mosque sermon about a man who went to England and took on a Western name to make himself new identity papers. "He is no longer Muslim, by right. He is nothing but a faithless hypocrite who denied his faith to serve his purpose." He went on with his story: "The man even had the nerve to write to an important mullah to plead his case, claiming he was still Muslim in his heart despite having adopted a non-Muslim name, but the mullah wrote back that Allah had created a special Hell for people like him. That's how it works."

The conversation changed abruptly, as it often did, and Nur Ali asked if Shahgofta had heard from the boy, meaning Iqbal.

"Yes, he called," she answered.

"When did he call? Was it yesterday or last week? Did you speak with him personally, or did someone else tell you about their conversation? Did you tell him to call his father? Has he been in touch with his wife?" He hardly paused to take a breath, and added accusingly, "I tell you everything I hear from everyone, but you, you withhold information from me. Why am always the last to know?"

Nothing irked him more than having his position as *qaida* compromised by feelings of alienation and exclusion. The anger swelled in him, and he had no choice but to let it. The anger kept him alive, kept him moving forward.

"I tell you what I know," Shahgofta replied defensively.

"And what news do you have of the village?" he continued interrogating his wife, perhaps forgetting that he had already asked her.

"Our sisters at home said it's still raining hard, and that the path down to Khwaza Khel has turned into a stream. No one can leave the house any more. People say the river is rising, and that some of the bridges are impassable."

"Allah!" sighed Nur Ali, pressing down on the pain in his lower back. "We are being punished for something."

"Pack of Newport 100s," the voice of a man wearing a hoodie brought him back to the reality of his surroundings.

"ID?" He had been trained to ask this in the case of cigarette purchases. "Okay. Eight, thirty." He took the man's money and gave him back change from the register. "Have a nice day."

"It has started to rain here, too," Shahgofta, who had been listening, pursued her response, "and we're all cramped inside the apartment."

Now the knot churned more fiercely in the *qaida*'s stomach because he knew there was nothing he could do to address this calamity. God's wrath was adding to his curse on them. He removed his hand from his lower back and began to frantically scratch the sudden itch that had erupted again along his arms.

7-ELEVEN

The next night, Nur Ali checked in for his night shift, and went into the back room to perform his prayers, as he did every night. Mo, the loud Moroccan, was temporarily back, working in the store to help with the evening rush, and was on until nine. Michael was there, too, and was staying till midnight. When Nur Ali emerged after his prayers to join them, the two were engaged in a lively conversation.

"I hate it when other Pakistanis I meet ask me why and how I came here," said Michael. "It's even worse than when Americans ask me the same question."

Nur Ali felt the same and said so. Swat Pashtuns and Christians were both minorities in Pakistan.

"If they even suspect that you came here to get married," Michael continued, "they look down on you. I always say that I came here on my own with a student visa," he added, but then shifted to what he really wanted to talk about. He had just met a woman and wanted advice from Mo as to how to make the moves on her. Nur Ali, having never interacted with any women beyond his own wife, and certainly never with any American women, avoided the conversation by getting up to make fresh coffee. But he listened nonetheless and continued to do so as he next put on a fresh batch of hot dogs and restocked the cooler shelves.

"What's her name?" asked Mo.

"I don't know," stammered Michael. "I don't ask. And I'm afraid to tell her I'm Pakistani. You know how people here are afraid of Muslims and especially Pakistanis."

"Not always," chimed in Mo. "Look at Niaz, who works for the cable company. He goes house to house and manages to have sex with hundreds of horny women clients alone at home. Or he charms them while on the job, and they invite him to return later. He's Pakistani and has no problem."

"I'm not like Niaz," said Michael. "I'm interested in something a little more solid and longer lasting. This woman is Christian, like me. She's Spanish."

Mo, who tended to be more like Niaz, and envied the possibilities that the cable company job offered, nevertheless toned it down for Michael. "Okay," he said, "you could text her, and establish casual communication for about a month. Keep it real easygoing, like 'How was your day?' or 'What are your weekend plans?' Give it about a month, and see where it goes."

Nur Ali, who had been listening to this dialogue in English, couldn't resist being the wise, conservative advisor. "I just know we have to prepare for the afterlife," he said to Michael in Pashtu, "and do our best while on earth. God tells us this. Regardless of our wealth, class, or position, we must do our best and accomplish our utmost. God has enough water for all believers. You do what you think is right, Michael."

This was Nur Ali's fundamental Muslim belief, which he had been taught growing up in his Swat village. It had followed him throughout his life and travels, and continued now to guide him. He thought it appropriate to share it with Michael.

But Michael did not want to talk philosophy. He preferred Mo's advice and wanted to continue talking about women and how to approach them.

"Do you remember watching women's feet in Pakistan?" he asked Nur Ali, but in English to include Mo. He didn't wait for a response but proceeded to tell Mo and Nur Ali—translating at times into Pashtu for the older man's benefit—about a dream he had recently had where he saw hundreds of women's feet appear in nanoseconds from under their burqas and chadors as they walked through a crowded bazaar.

This brought a sparkle to Nur Ali's eyes, as his mind's eye shot back to his own experiences.

"You know," the old exile laughed, "when we were adolescents, my brothers and I sometimes used to travel north to tourist towns like Madyan or Bahrain in Swat, where lots of men and women walked the street. We would sit on the side of the street and look at women's feet as they walked by, and if one of them stood still long enough, we could get a long look and guess all about her. Even though her feet were all that we could see under all that veiling, it was highly entertaining, and we compared notes on our assessments!"

"That's right," chimed in Michael enthusiastically. "I used to watch women's feet as they got on and off buses in Peshawar. You could always tell their wealth by the kind of sandal they wore, if it was plain plastic or fancy sandals from the Batta shoe store. Afghan women wore those black rubber slip-on shoes for rain and mud."

"Yes," concurred Nur Ali. "We looked at skin tone on the upper foot, at the back of the heel to see if it was smooth or dry and cracked, and on fingers if we chanced to see those. If the skin was dark, we figured they came from the south; if it was light, we knew they were Pashtun. And we looked at the toe nails. If they were shaped and painted with polish, we knew they were rich. Our native Swat women had large coarse feet, often muddied, with henna on their nails, and always wore cheap plastic sandals."

Michael sighed, "I wish it were that easy to evaluate women in America. Here they expose so much more for us to see and judge by. And the fact that we can openly talk with them makes it easier and harder."

Mo, who prided himself on his wealth of experience over his two friends, added his own personal anecdote. "When I first came here, and my English wasn't as good, I met a girl and asked her name. She told me 'Hooker.' So I thought this was her name, and one night I was looking for her in the same area of town I met her, and asked other people, 'Where is Hooker?' They laughed at me and said they were all Hooker."

This produced loud laughter from Michael and Mo, after which they explained it to Nur Ali, who had understood neither the humor nor the English.

Amid this good humor, which temporarily distanced the men from their personal agonies, the phone rang, bringing them back to reality. It was Momen Khan reviewing their schedules and list of duties with each in turn.

"By the way," their boss casually announced, "the IRS is pressuring employers to stop paying salaries in cash. I'll have to pay you by check, and as employees you'll be obliged to report your income and pay taxes."

Nur Ali cried out, "There won't be anything left! What's the point of working if I can't even provide for my family?"

In his fifteen years in America, Nur Ali had never paid taxes. He knew he was being underpaid but accepted this in return for not having to declare anything or pay taxes. Most of the Swat Pashtuns he knew, and for that matter, most immigrants and exiles, legal or illegal, remained under the radar. They spent much time comparing how hard they worked and how little they were able to make and send home, but it was worth it if they could remain unnoticed.

"I already make so little," moaned Mo.

"You only worked fifty-three hours last week," responded Momen Khan. "If you had worked seventy-two, you would have made more money. Look at Nur Ali. He consistently works eighty-four hours a week, week after week. If there is life, he'll go home a rich man."

Momen Khan, like many Afghans, had replaced the habitual phrase, "God willing," with "if there is life," which had come into usage in Afghanistan in the 1980s during the Soviet occupation, when everyone had experienced at least one war-related death in their family, and lived with the imminent possibility of death.

Despite the complaining, a few short hours later, Nur Ali gave his son, Naser, permission to purchase a camera for himself when the rain subsided, if that's what he really wanted. He had just paid for a new computer, and now the boy wanted a camera. The *qaida* remained the ultimate provider.

PAKISTAN NOW

"Salam alaykum."

"Walaykum salam, Lala." It was Mahmad Ali, Nur Ali's brother.

"How are things there?"

"Fine, fine."

"Is my son okay? How about my daughter-in-law?"

"Fine, fine."

"Any more intrusions by the army?" Nur Ali didn't often hear from his brother and was trying to guess at the bad news he could be bearing.

"No, things are good on that front," Mahmad Ali's words began slowing. "We have other things to worry about right now."

"Yes, I heard the rain is really bad," agreed Nur Ali. But he also had other things on his mind. "Is my boy with you? And how are the women faring at home?"

Both of Nur Ali's brothers, Mahmad Ali and Sardar Ali, as many other adult males from Khwaza Khel, were still hiding out in the mountain away from the village, fearing arrest and persecution while the Pakistani army pursued their raids in search of Taliban sympathizers. They were still searching for Iqbal, wanted for murder and Taliban support. The three of them occasionally took turns to trek to the compound for supplies and to check on the women.

"Things are okay," replied Mahmad Ali, "but the rain is not letting up, and the river is beginning to rise. Lucky for us, the house is far up enough from it that the water levels should not reach us. Our biggest worry is landslides. But the road along the river is closed, as are some of the bridges. It's a mess. As if we hadn't been through enough last year with the army destroying our villages and homes, this year the rains are pounding what's left. We're lucky we have our cell phones."

Nur Ali began scratching his arm vigorously. He could feel the knot tightening in his stomach. As he inhaled a deep breath of air, he told himself, *Stay in control. Order has to be kept.*

The road winding up the valley alongside the river was the only road connecting Peshawar, Lower Swat, and Upper Swat. If the bridges crossing the river at various intervals were disabled, it would completely isolate the communities and hamlets on the western side from the commercial towns and markets along the road on the eastern side. The bridges were pedestrian for the most part, hanging slatted bridges over raging waters. Nur Ali's thoughts raced to the crossings farther north along the river, the platforms that hung from a cable, in which the crosser pulled himself across using a pulley system. He became fixated on the bridges' condition during the devastating flood of 2010, as he blindly groped for news from everyone. He continued to scratch, then abruptly froze at his brother's next sentence.

"I need to discuss something with you," Mahmad Ali continued. The tone behind his words was hard, forceful, the same as it had been when he had usurped Nur Ali's authority in the matter of his first son's wedding. The *qaida* listened intently, holding his breath.

"So, I think it's safe enough for most of us to move back down to the compound, especially with the women alone there and all this rain. I came down yesterday, and I'm going to stay permanently. I'm moving back to the house. Your home, on the other hand, is in shambles. The army has broken it down, and the Bearded Ones have stolen everything from it, even the steel beams to sell in the market. The roof is leaking, and the mud walls are starting to cave in. You haven't been here in years to maintain it, and now that Bibi has moved to Karachi, followed by your oldest son, there is no one here to fix anything. And the boy can't move back here. Chances are, you'll never come back here to live. The government won't allow either of you back here to build it up, and it's just falling apart. I'm proposing to knock down the wall separating our two houses, and take over your house, incorporating it with mine."

Nur Ali stood frozen, too stunned by this news to respond, too astounded to resume his frenetic scratching. The pangs brought on initially by a need to make sense of the disastrous deluge of information and to make order from the chaos at home, were then doubled with the heated wave of rage that now surged through his body.

"Uh-huh," was all he could stutter, and then he managed to voice the words: "I'll get back to you later. I have to take care of business just now."

The *qaida* stood staring into space but was abruptly brought back to the reality of the 7-Eleven when he caught a shoplifter and angrily chased him from the store. Feeling oddly calmed by the local disturbance, he called Shahgofta.

"Salam alaykum. Were you sleeping?" Nur Ali heard a hint of fatigue, perhaps a slur, in his wife's voice.

"Walaykum salam. No, no." Even if he did awaken her, she never admitted to it.

"Is everyone alright?" He didn't wait for her reply. "I spoke with the village. Everyone there is okay, but it's raining hard, and the river is rising fast, flooding the lower areas. The road and bazaar are closed, and I'm worried about the bridges." In his apartment, Nur Ali followed the flood news on Pak TV. Even the American news was talking about it. Whenever he saw footage of people swarming to leave Swat, the exile squinted, leaning close to the screen, and scoured the images searching for familiar faces.

"Yes," she replied, "I've heard everyone is just sitting tight. Here, too, it's raining hard."

"Don't let the kids out for any reason. I told Naser to go buy a camera, but tell him I said no. I've heard that looting and street violence are on the rise in Karachi as the heavy rains and flooding are causing businesses to shut down. I worry about you so much when I see this stuff on the news, and even more when I can't get through to you. Hold on; I have a customer."

Shahgofta listened to her husband's broken English, not understanding the words. "Two-sixty-eight," he told the man. She recognized the numbers "two" and "eight."

The customer fumbled through his pockets and began laying change on the counter. Nur Ali finally addressed him, "If you no have, then no problem. But if you have, then give it to me."

"You have a good night," the customer replied as he turned to leave after paying.

"You, too," Nur Ali returned the polite exchange, adding in Pashto, "Screw you, asshole!" Suddenly understanding, Shahgofta cried out, "What! Why are you insulting me?"

"Oh, not you. It's just one of these people. If you only knew! You should see this guy... wider than three of me. People here are so fat they can't fit through doors or sit on the toilet. Even their babies are fat! And they're filthy. They keep cats and dogs inside their houses! They live in filth! And I still, for Allah's sake, I take pity on the poor, when they don't have enough to pay. It's just my habit. It's who I am."

Shahgofta sighed, and Nur Ali changed the subject. "I spoke with Mahmad Ali. He wants to take over my house. Said it's destroyed, and that I'll never return there anyway. He wants to knock down the wall between our houses and rebuild mine, connecting it to his own. Where does that dog get the nerve?"

"Well, you and I and our sons are gone from the compound, leaving no one to defend your position. Now he's coming in for the kill." Shahgofta's voice had the calm of thought in it.

The frenzied outrage from earlier welled up again in the *qaida*, his voice shaking. "What right does he have to threaten me? How can he take over our ancestral home when I am the oldest, the family *qaida*, and it's my home? When he himself built that wall years ago, I should have suspected he was breaking up the family. For years, I have been laboring, paying for everything he and his family needed.

"Yes," concurred his wife. "You paid to send his son to the best hospital for surgery when he needed it. And when his wife's father needed a kidney, you offered to give him your own."

"I paid for him to be sent all the way to the Agha Khan Hospital in Karachi," added Nur Ali, "because I knew that anyone going to Peshawar Hospital ran the risk of dying from infections. All along I expected he would pay me back when I returned home, and it would pay for my retirement. And now he wants to claim my home! How can he threaten me? Besides, I have too much support and too many people ready to avenge me if he were to kill me and become *qaida*."

An eye for an eye! Shahgofta knew exactly what her husband was referring to. Revenge and reciprocity lay behind and defined all their social relationships. Gifts, visits, inquiries, and even women as marriage partners were all exchanged on a reciprocal basis, just as family feuds extended over generations to preserve family honor. She said nothing, letting him rant.

"That's it," Nur Ali yelled. "Mahmad Ali is younger than I, and his intention to take over our ancestral home signals a clear breach in family ties and total lack of respect for tradition and for me. I swear, from this day, I am cutting all ties with my brother. Our families are now divided and openly hostile."

"Don't forget," warned Shahgofta, "that Sher Banu is still there, increasingly at odds with her aunts, who have found ways to shut her out and make her life miserable."

"I know," the qaida responded, flooded with remorse. "I told her earlier that she could move back into her parents' home, but it's been difficult to move her on account of all the rain." The *qaida* had to make a move. Anger would not resolve the issue.

"Try to contain your anger until the girl has been moved out," she warned him again, well aware of how a woman's life can be plagued by the wrath of her female in-laws.

But the harm had already begun. Until then Nur Ali had been able to call the house to check on Sher Banu and had found ways to channel money to her for her own and her children's needs. But when Mahmad Ali moved back into the compound from hiding, and took it over, Nur Ali could no longer call the house to talk with his daughter-in-law. One day, when he did call, Salma informed him that Sher Banu had moved back to her parents' house, using the flood conditions as an excuse. Nur Ali could not confirm whether the girl's husband had sent her to her parents, or if Mahmad Ali had chased her from the compound.

PAKISTAN NOW

It was before midnight that Michael called Nur Ali from the cooler for a call.

"Salam Alaykum," he began, in his usual manner.

"Walaykum salam," came the familiar voice he had not heard for so long. His heart surged with anguish, joy, and anger fused.

"My son has been born. Your grandson." Iqbal had come briefly to see his newborn before leaving for the Gulf with his uncle .

"Praise be to Allah," cried out the old exile, tears filling his eyes. "You will leave a son!" He thought of the celebration that would normally have been held, that would never be held now due to the flooding and the family's dire circumstances.

"Sher Banu will stay here with her parents for her forty-day after-birth period , and then I will arrange for her move to Karachi to be with Bibi," announced Iqbal.

"What about a name? I must share the news with your mother."

"I'll call her myself. What do you think of Aftab?" Iqbal laughed. "A ray of sun in all this miserable rain. He's as beautiful as a fairy."

"As a fairy!" cried Nur Ali. "Have you looked at yourself lately?" He took pride in remembering how handsome his son was when he had last seen him, his soft child's eyes shining.

As soon as power and phone lines were restored, family began calling the *qaida* in America to congratulate him on his newborn grandson.

7-ELEVEN

Anger at his brother mingled with the anxiety for his family's safety as the flooding in Swat worsened, creating a state of commotion within Nur Ali that he could not show from behind his store counter. His new grandson was now isolated from the family, and he had to listen to Sherry go on about her candy display in the store. He was cordial with customers. He perfunctorily went about each task: filling the cooler and slurpy machine, wiping down the counters, checking inventory and filling out order slips.

All the while, however, his thoughts remained fixated more on home and family than ever before and how he could resolve what seemed to be an increasingly hopeless situation. It wasn't as though he could take a day off to go handle any of it. His daily phone calls to family no longer served the purpose they once had, ordering and maintaining his universe. What could he possibly do from so far away to save his crumbling world?

He watched the news and talked with others at the mosque. Everyone had stories to tell about losses from the flood. Tonight, just as he emerged from cleaning and organizing the cooler, the phone rang. It was his friend, Bacha Gul.

"Good night, Brother. Are you okay to talk?"

"Yes," replied Nur Ali, welcoming the diversion. It was a relatively calm night, and at three o'clock a.m., there was no activity in the store.

"My town, Madyan, has been washed away," began Bacha Gul with a loud sigh. "There is nothing left. From Kalam, Bahrain, and Madyan in the north, all the way to Mingora and Charsadda in the south, there is not a single bridge left. They've reported nine hundred deaths, and hundreds of homes wiped out."

"I saw helicopters on the news," interrupted Nur Ali, "bringing in supplies to isolated areas, but it is devastating. This is God's greatest wrath upon us. You can see the contents from stores and tea shops in village after village just floating down the river."

"How much more can we take?" His friend slowed, searching for words. "How many more lives? Everyone is out of work, and schools no longer exist." He took a breath and continued, "What's the news in Khwaza Khel?"

Nur Ali wanted to save the news of his grandson's birth for a more opportune time. Instead, he added stories from his village. "Our family rice and corn fields have been washed away, as have what was left of the fruit orchards. Furniture, wedding jewelry, household and personal items are all in the river for everyone to see and anyone to pick up. Houses are turned inside out, and everything private is on public display."

"Have you been to the mosque? You'd weep to hear people's stories."

"Allah has brought this on to destroy the entire population. Do you know Mashang, the guy who sold his daughter to the Saudis for a lot of money some time back? His other daughter died."

"Yeah, yeah," said Bacha Gul, "he was in our clan, but distant. We didn't engage in any exchanges with him. His daughter had a son, a fat boy, a pretty useless guy."

Nur Ali and Bacha Gul exchanged stories of people they knew in common, now dead or homeless as a result of the flood, and Bacha Gul concluded, "We've all been dispersed, exiled to safe havens. All we have left in our power is to call and assure ourselves of our family's safe arrival to other relatives' homes. Our families and all of Swat have been displaced, if not by the Taliban and the Pakistani army, then now by the flood. There are no more Pashtuns, just a nation of homeless people."

"I don't know how much more I can take," agreed the old exile. "At this point, I have been away and missed my mother's death, both my sons' weddings, all my grandchildren's births, and my family's move to Karachi. And now to see them dispersed God only knows where."

In an abrupt return to local reality, Bacha Gul warned Nur Ali, "By the way, the store on the boulevard was burglarized earlier tonight, and word is they're on the prowl tonight. They shot the guy there and made off with the cash in the register and loads of cigarettes. The police came to warn me. Be careful."

"God preserve us all," Nur Ali said, and they hung up.

To calm himself and keep his emotions in check, the night manager began singing a very quiet melancholy traditional song from his childhood in a broken voice as his fingers gently pressed the numbers to the compound, looking at the calling card lying beside the phone, and waited for someone to pick up. He wasn't exactly sure why he was calling or whom he was expecting to speak with, but he knew there was some accounting to do.

He still had a good amount of money in keeping there. The gentle notes, half hummed, half sung, contained all the loneliness and alienation of the 7-Eleven night shifter. To his relief, Sabina, Mahmad Ali's wife, answered.

"Everyone is gone," she began crying. "My parents' house in the village was washed away, so I've been told to remain here until they return. It's awful. What's happening, *Qaidada*? There's no food. There's nothing. The government has said they will deliver rations, but we just sit and wait."

The head of the family felt helpless, still angry at his own brother, and could only mutter some words of consolation, reminding his sister-in-law not to forget Allah in this. None of them had been killed, and they must be grateful for that. He asked Sabina if she had heard that her husband was planning to take over his house, and from her vague response, he inferred her awareness. For years now, Nur Ali had been channeling a portion of his pay to Sabina, some to distribute to various family members, but most of it to put away for his return and retirement. The relations with Mahmad Ali now soured, Nur Ali sensed his money was suddenly at risk.

"You know you've been keeping some money of mine for me. Why don't you take out a portion to get you through this hard time, and keep the rest to give Sher Banu when you can," he suggested. "She'll need some right now, with her baby, and can take the rest to Bibi in Karachi."

"I'll do what I can, *Qaidada*," Sabina's voice calmed and turned cold. "But we are all facing hard times right now, and I don't know what your brother will let me do."

As he later explained to Shahgofta, "Sabina is ultimately under the control of her husband, and if he requests the money to cover expenses, she will be obliged to turn it over. With our relationship over, he could decide he needs that money."

For the weeks that followed the tragic flooding of 2010, there was little else on the lips of the entire Pashtun community in exile. Western Union lifted their fees to send money to Pakistan in an effort to show goodwill. Telephone lines were constantly busy and interrupted as everyone felt the need to reach out to family and loved ones, at least to know where they were. Throughout the US, mosques took up collections for flood victims. And every mosque bustled with stories of loss whenever Nur Ali went for prayers or to socialize.

"Did you hear about the guy from Mingora whose wife couldn't have children? He took another wife who bore him children, and brought her and the children over here, leaving the first one with his parents. They sent her out on an errand during the flooding, and she washed away, poor thing. Convenient way to get rid of an unwanted wife. She's probably better off, though, as she might have killed herself otherwise. There's no worse fate than to be a rejected wife, left at the mercy of in-laws. What a miserable life!"

"What about Omar from Mardan? He worked here sixteen years, and then got real sick. The doctor told him he had five days to live. He was headed home to see his family a last time, but his bus went off the flooded road and into to the raging river. After all that effort, he still died before being able to say good-bye."

"Do you remember Saber, the food-cart worker? He went home but couldn't find work. I'd heard he was planning to return. He was killed too."

"And the Imam from Deolai...they found his body in the river miles south of there and returned it for recognition and burial three days later in a pretty awful state of decay."   Stories like these were on the lips of every Pakistani exile for weeks.

Nur Ali recalled times when corpses had been transported back to the village to be properly prepared and buried by family. There had been a woman's body, back when he was a child at home, brought by bus from Lahore where she had died in the heat of summer. Nur Ali knew that his people did not believe in embalming, and that a speedy internment was mandated. But it was also imperative for the family to see the body and pay respects.

Nur Ali was still a boy at home the day he had gone with his mother and sisters to the woman's house, where dozens of women were assembled loudly wailing laments as they waited for the body to be carried from the Khwaza Khel bus stop up the mountain on a cot. When it arrived, the stench had overwhelmed him. He had chosen to remain outside in the courtyard rather than go inside, where the smells of death, sweat, tears, and the increased wailing were too much. The sight, combined with the sound and odor, had remained impressed in his mind forever. And he was reminded of this childhood experience as he thought now of all the corpses retrieved from the river and being returned to their villages in a similar state. Like every exile from Swat at that time, Nur Ali was filled with overwhelming anxiety and an urge to be home. He pressed those he spoke with to stay in touch with home.

"Is your home okay," Nur Ali asked another Swat Pashtun at the mosque.

"What home? I have no home left," answered the man.

"Do you call them?"

"What for? Our family line is finished. The brothers are all dispersed."

"You can't say that," Nur Ali tried to encourage him. "It's God's will. You need to call home. My home was destroyed. They took our land. But we're still connected. I know it's hard. My sons can't find work. No one is left in my village. We're scattered all over. But the same way we're being terminated, Allah will terminate them all." He wasn't sure if "them" meant the soldiers who ransacked his home or the Taliban who was terrorizing their valley. It didn't matter any more. In all his dealings, Nur Ali urged his fellow Pashtuns to remain connected with their families and to call often. He went so far as to reproach them if they did not.

PAKISTAN NOW

"Salam alaykum," he began his nightly conversation with Shahgofta.

"Walaykum salam." The flood had come and gone, and work at the 7-Eleven was ongoing. "What's new? I have lots of minutes tonight, so fill me in on everything. Has the boy called?"

As always, Nur Ali was referring to Iqbal, who, along with his uncle Mahmad Ali, had managed to leave Pakistan and join his uncle Yusuf Ali in Qatar to find work. Iqbal, recognizing that with his criminal record, he would not be able to work in Pakistan and would only continue to bring trouble for the home, had resolved to leave and try his chances in the Gulf . And while the government attention focused on flood victims and outcomes, it provided him an opportunity to escape without attracting attention. On his way, he also took his wife, Sher Banu, to Karachi to be with the rest of the family.

Although her family had survived the flood and remained in the village, the girl belonged with her mother-in-law and her legitimate family. Before she left, Nur Ali attempted to have her retrieve some of his savings from his sister-in-law Sabina when she went home to get her belongings, but to little avail. Sabina gave the girl a small amount of cash, claiming that Mahmad Ali had used most of it to pay for his own and Iqbal's airfare to Qatar.

Their other son, Ahmad, and his wife Rabia, were also still living in the Karachi apartment with Bibi. So Shahgofta now had her two daughters-in-law to help with the house work, two sons at home, and her grandchildren to fill her time. Ahmad had moved them to a slightly larger apartment to accommodate the six of them. Apart from her husband and one son, Shahgofta's immediate family was complete. She was content.

As for Nur Ali, he was no longer conflicted about where his money was going. He stopped sending anything to the village and sent his earnings through Ahmad directly to Shahgofta.

"Yes, he called last night," replied Shahgofta. "He hasn't found work yet, but he's alright."

"Good. As for the other two, Ahmad and Naser, why don't they ever talk with me?" complained the *qaida*. "What has all this exile gained me? My family is isolated from the group, and my own sons don't respect me. My heart burns continually in longing to see my sons. What has all this pain, suffering, and illness been for? Yesterday, I fell asleep content and even happy from conversation with friends here, and then Allah woke me and summoned me to remove my joy. I got up, prayed, and went back to sleep. Does this mean I am doomed to suffer forever?" He reached to scratch his arm through his shirt.

Nur Ali was in the middle of a deep sigh when he heard his granddaughter, Nazia, on the phone. "Baba? How are you, Baba? When are you coming home?"

"Soon, my child. Is my blanket ready?"

"Yes, Baba. And so are your clothes," replied Nazia.

"Are you helping your mother with your new brother?"

"Yes, Baba."

Nur Ali did not approve of the children calling him "Baba," and he asked Shahgofta when she returned to the phone what name appeared on her screen when he called.

"Abu," she responded.

"I can accept them calling me "Abu." I prefer "*Qaidada*," but I'll accept "Abu." Just don't let them call me "Baba." I don't like the name, and I don't want my grandchildren calling me that." Of course, not being there, he had no ability to correct them, and once a name was established in a child's mind, therethere was no going back to another.

Shahgofta had other pressing matters to discuss and changed the subject. "Your cousin, Nasif Jan, and his wife went to the village to ask for Naseema in marriage for their son. They brought some gifts and cash as good faith payment. There were six full suits."

"What! Have they lost their senses? Why didn't they call me? They can't just go marching into my house when I'm not there and request my daughter from my brothers! And I won't have them approaching you. This is something done between men, and women are not part of the discussion. You tell them nothing is going any further until they speak with me direct-ly. This is the most insulting thing I've ever heard! Is there no respect for tradition anymore?"

The young suitor's older brother called Nur Ali the next night, offering fifty-thousand rupees in cash and forty-five rupees in gold for Naseema . The *qaida* berated the young man, yelling, "This is for your father and me to discuss. It is not up to kids or women to decide. You tell your father to call me directly, and not to go making deals with my wife or my brothers. I'm the girl's father, and he's your father. I'd call him myself if I had his number. I'm not dead yet, and no one has any right to speak for me. They didn't even consult with me. There is protocol to follow!"

The rage and alienation that came in cycles swelled up in him again. When these waves of emotion came, they ran their course through his system till he became numb and was left hollowed out, as though the receding wave had sucked everything out of him. As the anger unjelled and flooded through him, the *qaida* thought back to Ahmad's and Iqbal's weddings, both of which he had missed.

When Ahmad had approached his father requesting to have his wedding arranged, Nur Ali had also exploded angrily: "Who would ever give their daughter away to someone who cannot even ask in person? And who will go ask for her and negotiate on your behalf if I'm not there? How can a wedding take place when there is no family to negotiate and prepare the rituals? Besides, you're asking for a girl who was previously engaged and whose fiancé died. Her family seems very willing to give her away, despite her vow not to marry anyone else. Who gives away their women so easily?"

Nur Ali had repeated this argument to everyone at the time, but in the end, feeling helpless and unable to participate as an on-site father would and should, he had consented to let his brothers negotiate on his behalf, and despite the *qaida's* absence, Ahmad was married to Rabia.

198

Nur Ali did all that he could during his daughter's entire engagement period, sending money for Shahgofta to prepare Naseema's wedding trunk—the clothes, shoes, and jewelry that would be hers alone. Shahgofta also prepared trunks of household items including kitchenware and bedding. Day after day, she reported to the *qaida* every rupee that was spent, and on what item. She also reported to him on every call, every gift that was given or received, every visit received or made. The lists kept him on the phone for hours, during which he performed his job behind the counter with increased rancor and irritation. Between the two of them, however, they needed to remember all this information for later reciprocation, and to know with whom they maintained good relations. Shahgofta could perhaps not write numbers, but she retained them accurately lodged in her memory, as she always did so adeptly.

These conversations were not only part of the *qaida's* need to know everything, but his desperate attempt to control the goings on in his house, with regards to his daughter, and also to somehow be there. He spoke with, or lectured, Naseema often, counseling her about the new life awaiting her, and how she would need to work very hard to gain the approval of her new mother-in-law, who would become the most important person in her life, her new Bibi. In the same breath, he also urged his daughter to stay in touch with her own mother and to firmly request permission for occasional visits home to be with her. All the while serving customers in his 7-Eleven, Nur Ali stood over Naseema's every move as reported by Shahgofta.

One day, he argued with his wife over giving Naseema permission to go to a neighbor's house to congratulate them for their new baby.

"Not over my dead body! Our daughter is engaged, and has no business being seen anywhere outside her mother's walls. You go," he commanded his wife, "but you will not allow our daughter to go with you."

And despite Nur Ali's outbursts over little issues such as these, he did not interfere further, and let the arrangements for Naseema's wedding proceed. Accordingly, she left the apartment in Karachi and returned to the village a bride. *Two sons and a daughter married without me* echoed continuously and sorrowfully in his mind.

As dictated by tradition, once a woman left her parents' home, they did not pursue her, and Nur Ali did not call either of his daughters after they were married . He spoke with them only if they were visiting his house, or if they called him, as they did to wish him a good holiday, or to congratulate him on the birth of a child. But beyond tradition, he frequently asked Shahgofta if the girls had called her, how they were doing, and if they sounded happy. The *qaida's* major concern was that their mothers-in-law were not mistreating his daughters.

7-ELEVEN

Shortly following Naseema's wedding, Nur Ali was talking with Shiriney one day in the store while she prepared it for inspection.

"How did your daughter's wedding go?" she asked.

"How would I know?" the employee sounded disgruntled. "I was not there. I barely participated in any of the negotiations or preparations. I have been exiled from all three of my children's weddings and the births of all my grandchildren."

Shiriney, always prepared and well stocked with personal stories, at once began telling him about wedding arrangements among her own relatives in Afghanistan.

"How do you manage it as a woman, being so far here in America?" With the awareness that his boss favored him, he spoke easily with Shiriney and respected her opinion.

"My cousin here in town, as a matter of fact," Shiriney began, "just arranged her son's marriage with a relative in Afghanistan. They talk every day over the internet where they can see each other as they speak. So, when the time came to select a bride for her son who is here, the potential brides in our village were all assembled for a video call, during which each one was pointed out, presented, and described to my cousin, who sat here scrutinizing and discussing them in turn with her relatives. I sat in on many of these sessions, wondering if I would do the same for my own son Adam. She asked about each one's age, weight, and height. She commented on their dress and skin tone. Following inspection, she then interviewed each girl about her housekeeping skills, preferences in food and clothing, her ability to make clothes, her completed schooling and ability to read, and her religious education. Obviously, she wanted someone from the family, but also someone compatible for her son who has grown up in America and will be bringing his bride to live with him here. This way, even from a distance, my cousin was able to control the choice of her daughter-in-law."

Clearly, this was foreign to Nur Ali, who did not grasp the array of communication technology beyond the store phone with a calling card or borrowing someone's cell phone. He had no visual or written contact with his family. Again, he thought about how his children's marriages had been arranged without his physical presence, and it pained him . With pangs of regret, he wondered how things might have been different if he had tried to learn this new technology.

PAKISTAN NOW

"Salam alaykum."

"Walaykum salam," responded Shahgofta. "How are you?"

"I'm not well," started Nur Ali. "Fifteen years of this, having to tolerate the foreign chatter and stand every night for twelve hours straight. I'm worn out. My back and legs hurt. If my back breaks, what good am I for work? One guy, he came to work here and walked out after two hours complaining of sore feet. I don't have issues like that, thank God, but my blood pressure goes up and down. My life is over. My father died at age sixty, and I'm fifty-three now. It's time I came home. I'm too old to be the sole provider."

"Why is your blood pressure up and down?" asked Shahgofta.

"What do I know? Are you a doctor, to be asking about my pressure?"

Shahgofta laughed. "I'm no doctor, but I'm curious as to whether it's fluctuating due to tension, anxiety, depression, or what?"

"It's because of depression. I had a dream last night that my father brought in bushels of beautiful peaches to the house, like he used to. He told me to gather up my patience. Then he teased me, saying I should not sleep fully because work was being done while I slept. But I don't feel strong enough to keep this pace. I'm tired of people reaching out just because they need money. My own sister called me in tears begging for money. She said her husband has lost everything and is unemployed, pressuring her to sell her wedding jewelry. I know she left the family and is no longer part of us and that I have no official responsibility to her, but what can I do? I have to send her something."

"That's a load of crap!" interrupted Shahgofta in a tone the *qaida* did not usually hear from her. "Your sister has all she needs, and don't you send her a dime." Her scolding broke off as she heard her husband start to babble in the language she didn't understand, and knew he was engaged with a customer.

"Please, take your stuff and go. This is store. Why you bring the dog? This is house dog; you keep in the house. The house dog not coming here!" Nur Ali did his best to contain his disgust at the dog and urged the customer to leave at once. Back home, dogs were not perceived as pets but as filthy creatures whose only purpose was as watch dogs. They never entered the house; the lucky ones were thrown scraps when there were some to throw.

He resumed his conversation with Shahgofta, letting his anger and disgust fly: "That bastard has the nerve to come in here with that dog! These filthy people keep cats and dogs." Nur Ali was on a roll: "They come in here and ask for things. In the middle of the night a woman will come in to beg."

"Do you give them anything?" asked Shahgofta.

"No; I'm fed up with it all. How little you understand! They live in filth. They keep cats and dogs in their home. Filthy people! And women have multiple men at a time!" Nur Ali switched back to address a customer.

Following the tension, the anger provoked by the thought of dogs, the customer's quiet social tea tone disarmed him, threw him too soon and too suddenly back into the mannered politeness Matthew had taught him to make his habit. He noticed his hands were shaking as he reached into the cash register to get the customer his change, then saw the hundred dollar bill. "No, sorry. We don't keep change." And then back again to Shahgofta: "Bastard comes in here wanting change for a hundred dollar bill. These people don't know mothers or sisters. They don't recognize anyone!"

"Do they have parents?" Shahgofta tried to put all this into the perspective of her own worldview. Not knowing mother or sisters was an expression used to refer to a male orphan who had grown up deprived of close female relatives and had therefore never learned to respect women.

"They have them," he responded. "They just don't recognize or respect them. A few do, but most don't." Even after fifteen years, Nur Ali's only interaction with Americans was from behind his counter at the store.

"You know," he resumed his earlier conversation, "I feel bad for my cousin who lost his home and family in the flood and now needs to resort to taking my sister's dowry to get by." As he spoke, he realized he was slumping, and arched his back to correct it, rubbing the cramped lower area with his free hand.

Once again, Shahgofta was quick to snap back. "He's just crying for pity, so you'll give him money! He's fine. He ran off with the others under pressure from the army. People today lie and steal and abandon their families. They borrow, disappear, and never reimburse a dime. Look at Nader; he took your money and moved to London. You never heard from him again, did you? Your cousin is lying. He just wants your money. Don't believe a word of what anyone tells you. They're all dishonest these days."

Shahgofta was beginning to accept that her husband would soon come home, and she was becoming less tolerant of his lavish spending on others when he should be more focused on filling his own coffers for their life together.

Nur Ali consulted with his wife on all financial matters, and she guided his decisions. He too was becoming increasingly anxious that the large amounts of money he had either lent or asked people to keep for him were at risk at this time of massive personal loss. Hadn't his own brother misappropriated his money to pay for his own financial needs?

Coupled with this gnawing feeling was the growing pressure from his immediate family to send expensive electronic gifts. Nur Ali felt he had become the family Santa Claus, one aspect of American culture he understood. His youngest son, Naser, badgered him for a new computer, camera, and finally an iPhone. And everyone requested a cell phone from him. When he spoke with his grandchildren, he would list off the items he had purchased for them: toy guns and cars, bangles, cell phones, and new shoes. And he played into his role on the phone with his grandson. "What should it be?" he asked the boy with sarcasm in his voice. "What should I send you: a car or a plane?"

The *qaida* began to feel that for those back home who had grown up without *his* presence, he was just the head of family, the provider of cell phones and money. It was the only relationship he had with his grandchildren, but at times it annoyed him, and he complained to Shahgofta that all they did was ask for things. He resented that his own sons were not beginning to take on the role of provider, at least for their own wives and children, never mind their parents. When Naser, who was still in school, got a part-time job, he teased him, "So, are you going to send me money now?"

And, in jest to his granddaughter Nazia one day, although it was said more to convince himself of his son's filial duty toward his parents, he told her, "Your dad is away working, so he can give his mother money."

Tonight, Nur Ali told Shahgofta the story of Aurangzeb Baba, the Moghul king, to illustrate the point that sons should take care of their mother rather than their father. "Remember that Aurangzeb threw his own father in jail in order to take the throne." Next, assuming his usual lectured way of speaking, quoted the local mullah, who had recently preached that their older sons would eventually drive out all the elders. Clearly, Nur Ali felt his time of retirement was nearing. He had done everything to prepare for it, was entitled to it, and was just waiting for his sons to take over.

"Is that all?" asked Shahgofta as they were running out of conversation.

"Why, are you in a hurry?"

"It's prayer time," she replied.

"Tell me what's new."

"There's nothing new. What am I supposed to tell you?"

"I have a lot of minutes. Just talk till the minutes run out," he pleaded with the despair he felt so often at the close of their conversations.

Shahgofta acquiesced. "Have you heard about the arrival of all the Chinese families in Swat who are opening laundromats throughout the valley?"

"Chinese, huh?"

"People with money are going there rather than to the river to wash laundry. Salma told me the girls bring thermoses of tea and sit for hours chatting while the machines wash the laundry."

But Nur Ali wasn't listening to her words as much as to her voice. He was suddenly filled with the horrifying notion that his wife was caught up in her distant world, and that he had become lost to her. He was desperate to nestle himself in that spot again, first in her thoughts and existence. Without thinking what it would sound like, he abruptly interjected, "Don't talk to anyone."

"Who do you want me to talk to besides you?" She was caught off guard.

"When you do your prayers, think of me BEFORE you start. I think of you all the time."

Nur Ali was feeling heavy-hearted tonight, homesick and alienated. He missed his wife terribly, but the only words he could articulate for all those emotions were: "No one gives a damn about me. No one calls to ask about me. This is the last time I call."

7-ELEVEN

"Hello, 7-Eleven," Nur Ali answered the phone at three in the morning.

Tonight it was Matthew, his former Pakistani Christian coworker who called from his fried chicken takeout.

"Salam alaykum, Mama. How are you?"

"Walaykum salam," answered Nur Ali. "Passing time in exile. The sky is above and the ground below. How's that new guy working out, the one I sent you?" He was referring to the newly arrived Pashtun he had placed.

"Oh, him? He ran out in the middle of his shift. He refused to do any cleaning. Let him go find better work!"

They spoke a while about their jobs and police reports, and the moment Nur Ali hung up the phone, it rang again. This time it was Bacha Gul.

"Did you go to the memorial service for Liaqat's wife yesterday?" he asked after their usual greetings.

"No," replied Nur Ali, laughing. "When I told my wife about him, that he had been here twenty-three years, she cried out that the man should be ashamed of himself leaving his wife behind that long, and that he has no right to lament her death now."

"On the other hand," continued his friend, and gossip source, "did you hear that Nuroddin just died here in town on the very day of his son's wedding back in the village?"

"What? No! Allah! God forbid! That's the sort of thing that can happen to a father who can't attend his son's wedding." Nur Ali recalled the pain he had felt over not being there for his own sons, and now, his daughter.

"Yeah, he just keeled over and died of heart failure. The wedding was cancelled, and people are going to pay respects tomorrow."

Nur Ali's mind raced to the birth of his first grandson, born to Ahmad in his absence. In his stomach now he could still feel the pangs of agony he had endured not only at not being there, but at his loss of leadership in the process of naming the baby. Ahmad had run several options for names by his father and other relatives, but they could not agree.

The name "Baber" was associated with a lunatic, claimed one.

"Asam" was hard to live with, claimed another.

The baby's uncles and grandfathers couldn't agree, and rather than defer to the *qaida*, the group had opted to let Ahmad name his own son. The incident, though minor, had marked the beginning of Nur Ali's loosening grip over the family.

"I swear, brother, if it weren't for my sons and grandsons, I would have no reason to go on living. No one deserves exile to the point where it kills them."

Within minutes of hanging up, Nur Ali was on the phone spreading the news around the community and gathering more information on the incident. The entire Swat community was aware of Nuroddin's death and would go for condolences the next day.

The community of exiled Pashtuns and other close non-Pashtun Pakistanis convened to pay respects for Nuroddin and give condolences at the funeral home. For these exiles, who on one hand vicariously suffered the losses at home, ethnic hatred in America drove them to depend ever more on each other, and this type of event reinforced the much-needed solidarity among them, reminding each one that they had the support of their expatriate community while away from home. It gave them occasion to physically show, by their attendance, their allegiance to the group, and not a single person failed to go. It was, in fact, the largest gathering of them Nur Ali had seen at once, and he showed surprise at seeing a few of them.

"I haven't seen you at the mosque," he addressed an acquaintance, Taj. "I thought you had gone home."

"You know, we have to attend events of joy and loss," started Taj. Attendance at these was crucial to Pashtuns as part of the network of reciprocity, just as the lack of attendance was a clear sign of hostility.

"Absolutely," conceded Nur Ali. "Back home, it's the first thing we say in describing people, whether we maintain that reciprocity of joy and loss with them or not. For example, my family and I no longer reciprocate with my brother."

He thought about each time there was a major event in his family and how he and Shahgofta spent days discussing who had called to either congratulate or offer condolences. They compared lists of calls, noting who had or had not called and used the information for purposes of future exchanges and relationships. With the vast distances separating exiles from their home, the phone had perhaps come to replace the physical visit, but the gesture, whatever the medium, was deeply rooted in tradition.

Taj added, "I'm the only person from my family here in America. We don't know Nuroddin's family, or live anywhere near his town, but as a Pashtun, it's important to come show our support, and to stay together. Times are hard, both here and at home for different reasons."

"Well," began Nur Ali, "I'm the *qaida* in my family. I have an obligation to attend each and every event in person or by phone. And they all call me in turn. There was once an old widow in my village whose son had gone missing, and for a long time I called her weekly to ask if he had come home. She finally announced that the boy had been arrested and imprisoned, but I continued calling to inquire after her son."

"You did all that from here?" questioned Taj, surprised.

"When my family passed on the news that the boy's body had been returned to the village from prison for burial, I called the grieving widow to console her and remind her that her son's death was God's will. The woman was now not only without a husband, but without a son to provide for her, left now to the mercy and whims of her in-laws, or the local community, if her in-laws turned her out as a useless burden. And this widow's community, in these trying times, was poor and struggling, hardly able to sustain another mouth. Consoling her was not easy."

"Allah!" Exclaimed Taj and a few other men who had gathered to listen to Nur Ali's story. "We all have stories of loss and homelessness. Allah is dealing a heavy blow to all Pashtuns." Once again, the sharing of despair served to seal and define the community.

Many situations were included in events of joy and loss, but the two most important were weddings and funerals. Funerals were broken down into first the in-house lament and condolence ritual before the official burial. When Nuroddin died on his son's wedding day, the family arranged to have his body sent home from America for proper burial. There was a Muslim funeral home in town which prepared the bodies according to tradition and made arrangements with the airlines to transport the corpse.

As the men in the funeral home continued to greet and embrace each other, they spoke about Nuroddin and wove stories of their own losses into the narrative exchange. Nur Ali lost control and broke down with another man, crying.

"What is left for us? What has Allah left for us? We are innocent and have done nothing wrong. I've let my beard grow so long people make fun of me. And yet, the Taliban and the army destroyed our homes and fields, our crops and fruit trees, broke down our doors and ripped the steel beams from our houses, letting them crumble. And then the flood took whatever was left. Families have been torn apart, dispersed and relocated. I'm one of the lucky ones who still have my sons. They take turns working in Qatar so that one always stays home with his mother. What do I need money for when I have children, bread to eat, and life? I talk with my family every day. No amount of money can replace that. It's meaningless. My family is all I have left to care about." He was preaching now, and a crowd had gathered.

"And as for all the infidels who have taken over our country," Nur Ali went on, "Allah will deal with them. They say on TV that our government is no longer Muslim. There are no Pashtuns left, only honorless people. Remember the story of Noah's ark, and what happened to all the infidels who didn't believe Noah as he labored to prepare? They got left behind to meet their fate. Believe me, this will come to be again. Infidels are the enemy of God."

Although Nur Ali and the others gathered at this moment of mourning voiced and wept over the communal loss, none made mention of their personal emotions, of the agonizing anxiety over the well-being of their wives and daughters, or of the pangs of separation they suffered each day they spent in exile.

Later, however, in one of their late-night talks to pass the hours behind their respective 7-Eleven counters, Nur Ali lamented to Bacha Gul, "What am I supposed to do? The longer I am absent from my village, from performing my own duties and attending my own events of joy and loss, I worry that I fall from the ongoing patterns of exchange and am dropping out of existence as a result."

"You?!" exclaimed his friend. "You remain so involved with home, more than anyone here. You're the last person to have to worry about not pursuing reciprocal exchange."

Bacha Gul's words were immensely heartwarming to Nur Ali, who was convinced that his absence from the exchange network lay behind what he perceived as a cultural exile, his own, as well as his family's, since he spoke and acted on their behalf.

PAKISTAN NOW

"Salam alaykum."

"Salam alaykum, *Qaidada*. How are you?" It was Rabia, who had just given birth to a baby girl, another grandchild for Nur Ali. For as much joy that was manifested at the birth of boys, a girl's birth was met with sorrow and kept quiet. When Iqbal and Sher Banu's son, Aftab, had been born, there had been an endless stream of joy, laughter, and congratulatory calls to the 7-Eleven, despite the floods in the village and the inability to celebrate.

Today, in contrast, only Shahgofta and Rabia called to matter-of-factly announce the girl's birth.

"Listen to me," began Nur Ali. "Girls are a gift from God, and we should not be upset or belittle what God gives us. You take care of that child. I'll come home soon and hold her." Beyond his lecturing words, the *qaida* yearned to be among them to welcome his new granddaughter into the world.

"Yours and Iqbal's blankets are always ready for you, *Qaidada*," responded Rabia . Bibi was performing her prayers, so Nur Ali took the occasion to share words with each daughter-in-law and grandchild tonight.

Sher Banu's daughter, Nazia, was going on four, and Nur Ali knew that her mother had been teaching her the basic prayers, so he asked her to recite them for him. Her recitation was full of hesitations, and as she forgot words, he, with the patience of a grandfather, filled the lapses and corrected her mistakes. But when Sher Banu got on the phone, he scolded her for not doing a better job with the child.

"You and your sister-in-law must teach your kids to pray. They don't know their basic prayer when I ask them. You must be insistent and make sure they know them."

"Yes, *Qaidada*," she acquiesced, knowing he was simply fulfilling his role as elder.

Having finished in his role of *qaida,* Nur Ali changed his tone with Sher Banu. In his heart, he loved speaking with his daughter-in-law and needed to show it.

"There's been a horrendous earthquake," he announced in a softer voice and proceeded to tell her about the recent incident in Haiti. As he did, once again, his attempt to be close yielded only reports and lectures when what he longed for was to see the expression on her face.

"Oh!" he heard her exclaim. "Where you are? Are you okay, *Qaidada*?"

"It's not here," he replied. "It is over in the other America, South America, the poor America on the other side of the earth." He shifted gear again, "Has your husband called you? Does he send anything for the family? And how is my grandson, Aftab?"

"Aftab is fine, *Qaidada*. And yes, his father sent us all new clothes for the holiday."

"Did he send a suit for me?"

"No, he didn't think you would be here."

A pain shot through Nur Ali's lower back, and when Shahgofta took the phone, he started in right away. "So, my son sends holiday gifts to every-one, and doesn't send a gift for his own father?! In all the years I've been away, have any of you ever sent me a single set of clothes or a single blanket for any holiday, wedding, or birth? What about me?"

"You wear those people's clothes, not ours," responded Shahgofta.

"Not in the house, I don't. I don't wear pants when I'm alone at home. I wear the same suit I left with. Don't I have a heart? Doesn't anyone think of me for anything besides money? I had a dream last night that you and I were slaughtering chickens for the holiday, and an enormous weight over-took me, and I fell over with the chickens."

"What a beautiful and insightful dream!" exclaimed his wife.

"Maybe for you, it is. Not for me. I woke up in a cold sweat. You know nothing about me and my life here. I don't look like when you last saw me. I've lost a lot of weight, you know. My body and my whole appearance have changed. People say I've gone mad."

"How so?" she queried with a raised eyebrow he could not see.

"Fifteen years of standing twelve hours a night wears on a human body. You haven't seen me. You can't understand the change. How about you? Is your body still like it used to be? Have you gained weight?"

"I've lost weight."

He shifted mood again. "Don't worry," he said more softly. "God will make you fat again."

Like most Pashtuns from the rural areas and mountains, Nur Ali favored large women. It was a sign of strength and good health. Thin women were considered less capable of enduring the physical labor it took to run a house and raise children. "Dry" and "brittle" were terms used to describe a thin woman.

"Have you become dry and brittle?"

"Don't insult me," she retorted.

"Take a guess if I still have my beard," Nur Ali continued. "How would you know if it disappeared? Go on, guess!"

"Knowing you," she retorted, "of course you still have it."

Nur Ali broke out into a broad smile. "You're right. God and the Quran say that men should wear beards."

"Lots of men here have shaved their beards," Shahgofta added. "Ahmad shaved his."

"What? My own son? Wait till I talk with him!" The playfulness had left his voice, and the *qaida* was back, attempting to sound in control of his family.

In an attempt to stop her husband there, Shahgofta abruptly announced, "I have to go cook bread for the meal."

But Nur Ali was not ready to let her go. "How many breads are you making tonight? Did you count one for me?"

"Why would I? You're not here. Do you want it dry?"

"Dry will be fine. I'll be home soon." His soft tone had returned, as did a strong wave of homesickness.

"For three years now, you've been saying you'll be home soon. I've prepared rice and bread for you so many times, and kept clothing and your blanket ready, but you never come home. Why would I believe you this time?"

"I went to see my lawyer about leaving," he explained. "I told him I want to drop my petition for asylum and return home. He tried to warn me that the threats that existed when I left would not have dissipated, and that I remain wanted by the government of Pakistan. I told him I understood. Then he asked why I had come to America in the first place, and I told him it was for work and money. He explained that I could not return for at least ten years, and I told him I wouldn't live another ten years. People have to do what they must in life, and meet their obligations. In the end, home and family are all that count. I explained to him that my duty here is over. My new duty is to take care of my wife and be by her side."

"I'll keep your clothes ready, then," she replied.

"And a bed. I hope I don't have to sleep on the floor when I get home. I don't do well on the floor, you know."

There was silence on the other end.

"Talk to me," Nur Ali pleaded with her, desperate to hold onto the illusion of being connected.

"What should I say? There's no other news."

"Anything. You know everything about everything and everyone, and you don't tell me. Just keep talking till the minutes run out." And a few seconds later, he added with exasperation, "Wait, I have to deal with a customer."

A teenage girl had just run into the store, crying. She told Nur Ali she was being chased, and she begged to use the phone. "I'll call you right back," he told Shahgofta then tried to calm the girl.

"You no cry," he urged her. "You no cry, okay? I lock door until police coming." The girl was shaken and just wanted to call her mother to come get her. And when she did reach her mother by phone, she cried, "Mom, just come get me. This weird-looking guy who works here let me use the store phone. But Mom, he smells bad and can't even speak English. I don't trust him. Please come, Mom."

Nur Ali understood the girl. *And I interrupted my call for this?*

PAKISTAN NOW

It was still early in the evening when an elderly man entered the store, pushing his own wheelchair. Michael and Samuel were still both on shift, and Nur Ali allowed himself to watch the man, expressionless, as he navigated his way through the aisles. After the man had completed his purchase and left, Nur Ali approached his coworkers.

"Do you think he's alone? Does he have a family to feed him and help him bathe?" he questioned them.

"I don't know, replied Samuel. Maybe he's homeless and spends the night on the street or in a shelter."

"He didn't smell like anyone helps him bathe," added Michael.

God forbid!" sighed Nur Ali. "God forbid we end up like that."

Later that night he recounted the visit to Shahgofta, adding, "Thank God I have a family, and that I won't be left alone like that . If I can't walk, you'll take care of me. And if you aren't there, then my daughters-in-law will see to me and help me clip my toe nails when I can't reach them."

PAKISTAN NOW

Unable to find a job in Karachi, Ahmad had gone to Qatar where both he and his brother, Iqbal, were now working as drivers, and Na'im's nephew, Yusuf, who lived in the same building in Karachi, kept an eye on the women along with Naser. Mahmad Ali was also in Qatar with the boys, and whenever Nur Ali spoke with his sons, he told them, "Just go about your business and don't pay any mind to your uncle. We have nothing to do with him anymore."

Iqbal and Ahmad did not understand or agree with their father on this issue and pleaded with him repeatedly to let bygones be bygones, and to mend the relationship between him and their uncle. "The family compound is no more," they tried to explain.

But Nur Ali held fast. "You should always remember that it's about more than your uncle's attempt to take over our compound. He used my savings to get himself and you out of the country."

Despite his son's pleas that their move had been the best option for them, the *qaida* refused to make amends with Mahmad Ali. He resumed warning his sons to keep their distance. As far as he was concerned, the family was irreparably divided.

After notifying his attorney of his intention to rescind his petition for asylum, and of his desire to return home regardless of all conditions, Nur Ali started planning his return. He consulted with his brother, Sardar Ali, about starting a business and purchasing some land together to build a house for both their families. Sardar Ali, his only brother to have remained in the village, agreed and called his brother daily to report on real estate prices in Swat. They would sell the dilapidated family compound and start anew in Khwaza Khel, building a two-story concrete home. They especially looked for real estate with retail space on the ground floor and living quarters above for both families. Prices were high, but Nur Ali still believed he had a lot of equity built up in the way of monies he had sent or lent to various family members, and it was time to start claiming it back and securing his return and retirement .   After all, what else had all these years of exile been for? He began to contact all the relatives with whom he had entrusted his hard-earned money for safe keeping over the years. The family would once again be united, living and working under one roof in Swat. His back hurt less these days. Unknowingly, he had stopped scratching himself. And the knot in his stomach, though still there, didn't swell as dramatically.

One night, Nur Ali told Shahgofta he had dreamed that they were eating honey together, and that this was a sign they would soon be together in good circumstances. He spoke increasingly about coming home and asked his children and grandchildren what they wanted him to bring them. He told Shahgofta, "When I get back, I don't want to add to your workload. We'll cook rice in the morning, and I'll just have one meal a day."

"I've been dreaming of packing," he reported to her one night.

"You don't need to bring home any of your old clothes." She knew he still held on to the clothes and a blanket he had left with fifteen years ago.

"Leave them all behind. There are new clothes for you here, and you'll have no need for those old rags."

His calls with Shahgofta of late were all sweetness, like the honey of his dream, but as he began calling his other relatives, a different reality slowly unfolded.

"Salam aleykum, Peda Mahmad."

"Walaykum salam. Is it you, Nur Ali?" answered the voice on the other end, surprised to hear from his exiled relative after so many years. "How are you? Have you decided to settle in America?"

"No way! As a matter of fact, I'm coming home. Do you recall the money I loaned you a few years ago to pay for your son's wedding, which you promised to pay me back when I needed it? Well, the time has come. I'm coming home, and I need the cash now to purchase a new house to resettle in Khwaza Khel."

"Oh, brother. I'm so sorry. With the flood, I lost my business and was never able to earn the money back. I have absolutely nothing to repay you with. On my father's grave, I apologize."

One by one, he called cousins, inlaws, village friends, only to find that one after the other had spent what they had been entrusted with and had nothing to repay him. Each had a story to tell: a family emergency, a loan to pay, a business to buy, a home improvement, a wedding, a surgery, unemployment, loss from the flood. The list went on over three nights of calls. One had even forgotten that Nur Ali had sent him anything at all. Even his most trusted cousin, Na'im, claimed he spent the money moving and establishing Shahgofta and the family in Karachi, and had nothing left. Despite how involved the *qaida* had remained all these years, despite being the great provider to his extended family network and friends in the village, despite his attempts to stay connected by phone, he discovered over the three days that people had become comfortable with the belief that he would not return and would never demand anything back from them.

One of the many calls he made was to his older daughter, Shahgul. When her husband, Liaqat Ali, had started to run out of money to make their house payments, Nur Ali had sent Liaqat Ali a considerable amount of money over a two-year period to help out, with the understanding that his son-in-law would pay it back in time. But quite the contrary happened, and the young man was once again so penniless that he was forcing his wife, Shahgul, to sell her wedding jewelry.

Nur Ali, outraged, cried to his daughter. "We sent you off with that jewelry for yourself! The only thing a woman has any claim to in life is her jewelry, and she should never get rid of it!"

Night after night in the 7-Eleven, call after call, he grew increasingly obsessed with rage and despair. Back pain, scratching, now all returned and were more pronounced than ever. He felt he was falling apart at the seams: He had sent over forty-million rupees home, expecting financial security, and it had all vanished . The exile's dream was shattered in the course of those three days.

On the fourth night he shared his grief with Shahgofta. "No one knows you anymore," he said, "when it's your turn to need."

7-ELEVEN

"Hello, 7-Eleven," Nur Ali answered the store phone.

"Salam akaykum, brother." It was Bacha Gul, his most reliable news source. "There's been a plane crash in Karachi, with lots of dead and missing. There was a handful from our area. Remember the Hindko family in Mingora? They ran a business matching up households in Swat who wanted to sell their girls into marriage with wealthy Saudis who paid handsomely for them? I think the father and son were killed in the crash. And the Khans from Mardan."

"Allah!" half cried, half gasped Nur Ali upon hearing the news. "I remember when our Swat girls were being sold to Saudis in the '80s and '90s. We had a few in our village go that way. You'd suddenly see a lot of lavish spending, and then the women would visit and learn that a daughter had been sold. God forbid!" Swatis used the marketing terms – buying and selling- to refer to their girls who were married off to outsiders, or foreigners, for high bride prices.

"Did they ever sell to the Afghans?" asked Bacha Gul. "We had a lot of them up in Madyan. They came and rented houses. Residents vacated their homes during the summer and moved in with relatives in order to make money renting out their houses to Afghan refugees who could afford to escape the heat of the Peshawar camps."

"No," replied Nur Ali, "we never had that. Khwaza Khel was never a tourist site like Madyan or Bahrain. Only locals, or folks from across the river, ever came to our market. Even the Saudis never stopped off in our village. But we'd hear about them, and people in dire need would go seek them in the bigger towns." Nur Ali changed the subject, wanting to address his own need. "By the way, is Mir Zaman going to New York any time soon? I'm running low on *naswar.*"

Nur Ali was remnant of a generation that was addicted to *naswar,* the to-bacco-snuff he had seen all the older men use while he grew up in Swat. Generations following him had turned to cigarettes instead and claimed that only "old men" used the product. As he spoke, Nur Ali rolled a little ball of the remaining *naswar* he stashed in its metal box, and carefully wedged it between his gum and lower lip on the side. He would let it sit there as he salivated and spat into an empty coffee can he kept hidden on a shelf under the counter. There was no local source for his supply, and he was strongly addicted.

"I'll ask him," replied Bacha Gul. You want a kilo?"

"Yeah, I'll take a kilo. I always sell some around town."

After his conversation with Bacha Gul, Nur Ali made several calls, one after another in a meticulous order fit for a *qaida,* to other Pashtuns just to verify the report of the plane crash and get more information on the names and origins of those dead. As always, he was fiercely driven by his need to be as informed as possible, and to then project and pass on his knowledge of events at home, posing as the ultimate authority . With each detail he gleaned, he progressed to the next call and acted shocked that his listener was not informed of what he himself had just learned.

PAKISTAN NOW

"Salam alaykum," started Nur Ali, announcing himself.

"Walaykum salam," replied Shahgofta. "Who is speaking?" She was in a good mood.

He immediately tuned in to his wife's light pitch that matched her humor and good mood. "I don't have a name," he replied, playing along with her.

"Who are you looking for?" He thought he heard a stifled giggle and smiled.

"You don't recognize me?"

"No."

"Nur Ali."

"I don't know anyone by that name," she said truthfully: She never had nor ever would address her husband by his proper name.

"Aftab's grandfather," he responded, and they both laughed outright at their mutual joke.

"How's your girlfriend?" Shahgofta was teasing him about his coworker, Layla, whom he had spoken so highly of on many occasions.

He chose not to address her question, deciding it was time to get serious.

For two days now, Sher Banu had complained that Aftab was suffering from an earache. Nur Ali dove in with his usual list of questions: "Is the boy's ear infection any better? Have you heard from the boys?"

"Didn't they call you just yesterday?" asked Shahgofta.

"I asked if they called *you*." It was Nur Ali's turn to be playful with their words.

"They can't be calling us *both* of us every day," She replied.

He ran a check of her supplies. "Do have power and water?"

"Yes, there are fewer brown-outs here than in the village."

"Do you have oil, flour, tea, and sugar in the house? Do you have meat for tonight's dinner?"

He reviewed current food prices with her then finally arrived at what he wanted to report to her.

"I dreamed of a fifty-foot long bridge with nothing above it," began the exile, "and just a black void below, like an ocean or a grave. There were lots of slats missing. Three people told me to cross it. I asked them how, and they just told me to do whatever I had to. I set out and slowly inched across."

"What were the people like who ordered you to cross?" questioned Shahgofta.

"I forget what they looked like."

"Were they good or evil?"

"I forget. They were in black. I was afraid of them. It was a very beautiful dream. You need to tell it to the children."

"What else is new?" asked Shahgofta.

"I'm sick."

"Did you see a doctor?"

"No doctor can help me with this," said Nur Ali.

"Good. Then, it's nothing serious."

"You're rejoicing over my broken heart!" he cried.

And while the two of them bantered back and forth, a young woman who had entered the store stood at the counter, talking with her landlord on her cell phone: "They broke into my apartment and took all the money I had. I work hard every day, and now I can't pay my rent this month." As she began to sob next to Nur Ali, he momentarily told Shahgofta to hold on while he consoled the girl and urged her to stop crying, but she lashed out at him: "Back off, you Arab terrorist !"

As easily as these vile words escaped her lips, she was back to lamenting her situation with her landlord on her cell.

Somewhat bewildered by the ease of the young woman's stereotyping, but by now accustomed to insults at his expense, Nur Ali returned to his own conversation. "She's crying over her own fate," he calmly told Shahgofta. "They took everything from her house. People do that here; they break into homes and steal your money and belongings. God couldn't find more thieves in the entire world than there are here."

"Oh, yes He could," chimed in Shahgofta. "What about all those relatives you gave money to for safekeeping who just took advantage of your generous heart and have abandoned you?"

Nur Ali did not address that point. The sting of this girl's insult, however, did not override the initial derision that her predicament had sparked, and on which he remained focused.

"They're such bad people here. I've seen the entire world, except China," he said, alluding to his years working as a seaman, "and I've never seen people as filthy and wicked as here. Everyone has a story to tell of their home being broken into at least once. You can't walk the street without being mugged for whatever money or phone you're carrying." Nur Ali then added, "I've never done wrong by anyone." He wanted to distinguish himself from the foreign culture he assessed around him, more for his own benefit than Shahgofta's. "Even if I don't like someone, I am decent with them and act cordially toward them. This girl insults me for understanding her situation and wanting to help her. What is with this world? What is with these people?" He cast a glance at her and then determined not to look at the crude young woman again, hoping she would just leave the store.

Nur Ali shifted gears to a new, more immediate matter. He had sent some money via Western Union the day before and wanted to give the family the number and amount so Naser could go pick it up at the bank. But Shahgofta, incapable of writing down the numbers, had to call over Sher Banu for this.

"How many times did I tell you to pursue your schooling, and you never did?" he yelled into the receiver. "Now you can't even write down a number!"

After he exchanged greetings with Sher Banu—glad he had insisted that both his daughters could read and write—he gave her the money order number. He then inquired, as usual, after her children and her needs.

"Thank you, *Qaidada*," replied the young mother. "Aftab is still running a slight fever, but he's eating and sleeping alright."

Resorting to his *qaida* lecture mode, Nur Ali continued. "Remember to get along with everyone and do your prayers. I'll be home soon. Does your husband call and send you money?"

"Yes, *Qaidada*. We're all doing our best."

He then shifted off being *qaida* to relate some gossip he'd recently heard about two women who had recently burned themselves alive by pouring oil on themselves. In both cases, the husband had come to America and left his wife behind with in-laws in unbearable conditions. One was married to someone from Derrai, related to someone from their village. This was Nur Ali's way of showing concern for Sher Banu, checking that she was content and did not feel neglected by her husband. He had never forgotten what loneliness could do from the visit to the women with his mother as a boy of eight years.

"We bide our time and do what we must to prepare for the afterlife," he reminded his daughter-in-law. "You are in a good family and should not worry."

"It's alright, *Qaidada*," Sher Banu assured him. "Your son called to say he was coming home soon."

Nur Ali recognized the promises spoken by a man who could never come home, who would always support his wife and children from exile, but he offered no contradiction.

Sher Banu also informed her father-in-law that she knew one of the burn vicitms he had mentioned, and that it was in reality the woman's in-laws who had burned her and not a self-afflicted death. This revelation shocked Nur Ali.

"With her husband gone and his return negligible," continued Sher Banu, "she had become a burden and a useless mouth to feed." She paused. "*Qa-idada*," Sher Banu lowered her voice, "it happens a lot."

"Rest assured," the *qaida* told the girl. "No such thing will happen to you as long as I live."

Nur Ali did not wish to pursue this topic and abruptly asked, "Why doesn't anyone call me anymore?" But he knew the answer.

His expectations for returning home to a comfortable retirement now shattered, Nur Ali no longer responded to the cries of poverty and despair from relatives. He had turned away from being the wealthy *qaida* who was there to generously support one and all in their moments of need. He could only balance small payments home, while amassing enough to pay for his ticket home. He had a hard time explaining this to Shahgofta when she complained that she was low on cash. Relatives, meanwhile, knowing they could no longer count on him for support, stopped communicating with Nur Ali. The only person who remained faithful was his brother, Sardar Ali.

Shahgofta took the phone from Sher Banu and Nur Ali questioned her about their son, who had landed a job in Qatar and sent a care package of gifts home. "So, what did my son send with my name on it? A suit of clothes? Some cologne? A watch?"

"No, there was nothing for you," she said, "but he doesn't know you are coming home." Shahgofta regularly made excuses for the fact that neither of their sons sent anything for their father.

"Our sons are worthless!" Nur Ali cried. "I have labored in exile all my life, all for my children, and they do not speak to me or recognize me in my own house. It has all been for nothing! God knows my story. I've lost everything I had, my home, everything! We destroy ourselves for our kids, and for what!"

After he hung up, that night the *qaida*, alone in the store, sobbed deeply in the quiet night hours at the 7-Eleven, feeling more than ever the visceral pangs of isolation and worthlessness. He was grateful no one came in for coffee or cigarettes to witness his desolation. But he suddenly recalled a flood of memories that brought comfort: of waking up to the sound and sight of his mother or wife in the room preparing tea or fried bread, of someone else already awake and expecting him. In the quiet lull behind his counter, Nur Ali momentarily closed his eyes on the brightness of the store, and just soaked in the memory. He realized how terribly he missed that connectedness to others and how lonely he was. He reached with the fragile tendrils of memory to conjure up, at the very least, the smell of fried dough and freshly brewed tea.

PAKISTAN NOW

Recent events at the store did nothing to help Nur Ali's situation. Momen Khan had appointed a young new day manager, a young Afghan who spoke Dari and not Pashto, and who did not care for Nur Ali, his bearded appearance, bug bites, or body odor. He criticized him publicly and refused to allow him any prayer time in the store. He was Muslim, or so he claimed. Nur Ali doubted his faith; how could he not not appreciate praying, whether on or off store time? On the flip side, the man stole cartons of cigarettes, came in late consistently—obliging employees to remain long beyond their shifts—and invited his friends to sell drugs from the back room. Although Nur Ali reported this to Momen Khan and Shiriney, it was to no avail. Despite his corrupt behavior, he was tech-savvy, was boosting sales and running the business well. The bosses wanted to keep him on.

One day, the new day manager asked Nur Ali if he could borrow some money.

"I'm so sorry," replied Nur Ali, "but I sent my pay home yesterday. I kept just enough to cover my rent and food till next payday."

"I lent money out, and now I'm short," continued the young man. "And the guy isn't paying me back as I expected."

"Oh, I know how that goes," started Nur Ali. "People fail on loans all the time. I have a relative in Washington who needed money when his two sons were killed in a bus accident back home, so I lent him a small sum. This other guy also lent my relative some money, and then came to me looking for it because it was my cousin. I had to explain to him that it's just the way it goes in life. My relative never paid either of us back. That's only one example. I've sent over 1,200,000 rupees to various people back home when they needed to cover emergencies like bails, funerals, weddings, medical procedures, et cetera. And now, no one has a cent to pay me back. How do you think I feel?"

The manager looked at the old employee from wide eyes, and backed off for a while, but when Nur Ali told Shahgofta about the request, she warned her husband that his job could be at risk. She told Nur Ali this may be an indirect attempt to claim bribe money to keep his position. She was all too familiar with the corruption and bribery that made Pakistan function. And so was he.

The situation grew progressively more uncomfortable in the store. Momen Khan and Shiriney's son, Adam, had befriended the day manager and convinced him to let him sell drugs from the back room. Adam had grown up and gone to school in America. Although his parents supported and practiced certain aspects of Afghan culture in the home, they had not sent their son to the mosque for a religious education. They opted instead to have Adam grow up fully assimilated in American culture and not have to live the pull they saw their friends' children suffer as they struggled to satisfy the mosque and their American peers. He was Muslim by name but considered himself American first. In this case, the assimilation backfired. Adam was now a seventeen-year-old high school senior, embittered and confused about his own identity. He was a typical American youth who could only minimally speak his parents' language, Pashto. So he felt distanced from the immigrant community. Now, he also felt shunned by his American friends and classmates.

Adam had been very young when 9/11 occurred, so he hadn't noticed the change in attitudes toward Muslims in America, but by the time he reached middle school, he had suffered the wrath of ignorance from his American peers right along with the other Muslim students . Whereas he had never felt any different from them, he became labeled as "the Muslim," "the terrorist," and worse. He was lumped into an ethnic entity that became the target of misguided hatred—an identity he knew nothing about. Unjustly, he lost friends, lost his position on the basketball team, and lost interest in school altogether. Whereas his Afghan peers, raised to meet religious and social obligations of Muslims, convened at the mosque now for the youth groups and social activities provided there, Adam felt just as alienated from them as he did from his American peers. He began looking for a place to belong and feel welcome and ironically found it at age sixteen in internet chat rooms led by Muslim extremist recruiters. Bigotry and alienation in America set him on the path toward becoming the very thing they feared .

Because Adam's parents appeared to favor Nur Ali as an employee, and knowing that the old man disliked America and felt the same alienation he did, the youth turned to him as a sounding board, hoping even for an ally.

One evening, while Adam was in the store's back room and Michael was still at the front counter, Nur Ali took a break to go sit with the boy and play a paternal role. He always felt better when he could be the *qaida*.

"What are you getting out of this behavior?" he chose the most direct approach. "What do you have to gain from selling drugs? Do you need the money?"

"I do," replied Adam in broken Pashto. "I need money to get over and fight the jihad. I have found good people, people who welcome me for who I am, and who want and need me. They suggested that selling drugs was the quickest way to make that money."

"Do your parents know about this?" questioned Nur Ali.

"They don't need to know. I don't need their support or understanding. This is jihad, a duty, and duty requires no parental consent." Adam was certain and deliberate in his words. There was a glassy clarity in his voice that Nur Ali found disturbing. But this triggered Nur Ali's most passionate topic on which to lecture.

"Don't you realize that it's dangerous, that you are being seduced by hypocrites?" he asked, emphasizing the word hypocrites, "who just want your body to serve their war, to strap a bomb to yourself and die for their purpose? They have no more appreciation of you than your school friends do." Nur Ali was emphatic and stood, scratching both arms together in an agitated self-hug.

"You don't understand," Adam defended his position. "A martyr in combat gains the highest position in Paradise, and his immediate family gets the same. There are all sorts of benefits, including women and gold palaces. My friends guarantee that I can raise money fast by dealing drugs, and then be prepared to join them and contribute in person."

"They certainly have you seeing gold," replied Nur Ali. "Be careful not to become an infidel whose only purpose in fighting is money and rewards. Infidels are easily spotted and defeated." Even as he spoke, however, he felt that the youth was beyond convincing otherwise.

What perverted version of Islam is he following? Nur Ali worried to himself. This was not Islam, nor true jihad, which he had always learned was about self-control and inner mastery.

"Besides," continued Adam icily, "martyrs die a noble death with smiles on their faces. Their bodies don't decay but stay warm and smell of sweet musk and mint. Infidel corpses turn black and reek after an hour."

What nonsense! Nur Ali cringed. But he made one last stab at his efforts. "Listen to me. Your friends are the ones responsible for the unfair reputation we all have to live with. It's because of religious fanatics and extremists that we are all treated the way we are here. You are siding with them against your own community." From the young man's hard determined look, he could see that his words fell on deaf ears. He wondered if the young Afghan day manager was behind this, and whether he should alert his bosses. In the end, he had enough troubles of his own, and he decided to stick to his own problems, which were mounting by the moment and took all his attention.

7-ELEVEN

Recent events at the store did nothing to help Nur Ali's situation. Momen Khan had appointed a young new day manager, a young Afghan who spoke Dari and not Pashto, and who did not care for Nur Ali, his bearded appearance, bug bites, or body odor. He criticized him publicly and refused to allow him any prayer time in the store. He was Muslim, or so he claimed. Nur Ali doubted his faith; how could he not not appreciate praying, whether on or off store time? On the flip side, the man stole cartons of cigarettes, came in late consistently—obliging employees to remain long beyond their shifts—and invited his friends to sell drugs from the back room. Although Nur Ali reported this to Momen Khan and Shiriney, it was to no avail. Despite his corrupt behavior, he was tech-savvy, was boosting sales and running the business well. The bosses wanted to keep him on.

One day, the new day manager asked Nur Ali if he could borrow some money.

"I'm so sorry," replied Nur Ali, "but I sent my pay home yesterday. I kept just enough to cover my rent and food till next payday."

"I lent money out, and now I'm short," continued the young man. "And the guy isn't paying me back as I expected."

"Oh, I know how that goes," started Nur Ali. "People fail on loans all the time. I have a relative in Washington who needed money when his two sons were killed in a bus accident back home, so I lent him a small sum. This other guy also lent my relative some money, and then came to me looking for it because it was my cousin. I had to explain to him that it's just the way it goes in life. My relative never paid either of us back. That's only one example. I've sent over 1,200,000 rupees to various people back home when they needed to cover emergencies like bails, funerals, weddings, medical procedures, et cetera. And now, no one has a cent to pay me back. How do you think I feel?"

The manager looked at the old employee from wide eyes, and backed off for a while, but when Nur Ali told Shahgofta about the request, she warned her husband that his job could be at risk. She told Nur Ali this may be an indirect attempt to claim bribe money to keep his position. She was all too familiar with the corruption and bribery that made Pakistan function. And so was he.

The situation grew progressively more uncomfortable in the store. Momen Khan and Shiriney's son, Adam, had befriended the day manager and convinced him to let him sell drugs from the back room. Adam had grown up and gone to school in America. Although his parents supported and practiced certain aspects of Afghan culture in the home, they had not sent their son to the mosque for a religious education. They opted instead to have Adam grow up fully assimilated in American culture and not have to live the pull they saw their friends' children suffer as they struggled to satisfy the mosque and their American peers. He was Muslim by name but considered himself American first. In this case, the assimilation backfired. Adam was now a seventeen-year-old high school senior, embittered and confused about his own identity. He was a typical American youth who could only minimally speak his parents' language, Pashto. So he felt distanced from the immigrant community. Now, he also felt shunned by his American friends and classmates.

Adam had been very young when 9/11 occurred, so he hadn't noticed the change in attitudes toward Muslims in America, but by the time he reached middle school, he had suffered the wrath of ignorance from his American peers right along with the other Muslim students . Whereas he had never felt any different from them, he became labeled as "the Muslim," "the terrorist," and worse. He was lumped into an ethnic entity that became the target of misguided hatred—an identity he knew nothing about. Unjustly, he lost friends, lost his position on the basketball team, and lost interest in school altogether. Whereas his Afghan peers, raised to meet religious and social obligations of Muslims, convened at the mosque now for the youth groups and social activities provided there, Adam felt just as alienated from them as he did from his American peers. He began looking for a place to belong and feel welcome and ironically found it at age sixteen in internet chat rooms led by Muslim extremist recruiters. Bigotry and alienation in America set him on the path toward becoming the very thing they feared .

Because Adam's parents appeared to favor Nur Ali as an employee, and knowing that the old man disliked America and felt the same alienation he did, the youth turned to him as a sounding board, hoping even for an ally.

One evening, while Adam was in the store's back room and Michael was still at the front counter, Nur Ali took a break to go sit with the boy and play a paternal role. He always felt better when he could be the *qaida*.

"What are you getting out of this behavior?" he chose the most direct approach. "What do you have to gain from selling drugs? Do you need the money?"

"I do," replied Adam in broken Pashto. "I need money to get over and fight the jihad. I have found good people, people who welcome me for who I am, and who want and need me. They suggested that selling drugs was the quickest way to make that money."

"Do your parents know about this?" questioned Nur Ali.

"They don't need to know. I don't need their support or understanding. This is jihad, a duty, and duty requires no parental consent." Adam was certain and deliberate in his words. There was a glassy clarity in his voice that Nur Ali found disturbing. But this triggered Nur Ali's most passionate topic on which to lecture.

"Don't you realize that it's dangerous, that you are being seduced by hypocrites?" he asked, emphasizing the word hypocrites, "who just want your body to serve their war, to strap a bomb to yourself and die for their purpose? They have no more appreciation of you than your school friends do." Nur Ali was emphatic and stood, scratching both arms together in an agitated self-hug.

"You don't understand," Adam defended his position. "A martyr in combat gains the highest position in Paradise, and his immediate family gets the same. There are all sorts of benefits, including women and gold palaces. My friends guarantee that I can raise money fast by dealing drugs, and then be prepared to join them and contribute in person."

"They certainly have you seeing gold," replied Nur Ali. "Be careful not to become an infidel whose only purpose in fighting is money and rewards. Infidels are easily spotted and defeated." Even as he spoke, however, he felt that the youth was beyond convincing otherwise.

What perverted version of Islam is he following? Nur Ali worried to himself. This was not Islam, nor true jihad, which he had always learned was about self-control and inner mastery.

"Besides," continued Adam icily, "martyrs die a noble death with smiles on their faces. Their bodies don't decay but stay warm and smell of sweet musk and mint. Infidel corpses turn black and reek after an hour."

What nonsense! Nur Ali cringed. But he made one last stab at his efforts. "Listen to me. Your friends are the ones responsible for the unfair reputation we all have to live with. It's because of religious fanatics and extremists that we are all treated the way we are here. You are siding with them against your own community." From the young man's hard determined look, he could see that his words fell on deaf ears. He wondered if the young Afghan day manager was behind this, and whether he should alert his bosses. In the end, he had enough troubles of his own, and he decided to stick to his own problems, which were mounting by the moment and took all his attention.

PAKISTAN NOW

"Salam alaykum."

"Walaykum salam, Baba. How many more days before you come home?" It was his granddaughter, Nazia.

"Very few, child." *Why was she still calling him Baba!* "How is your brother, Aftab?" He decided not to lecture about his title today as other, more troubling things were at hand. Over the past few days, what had started as an ear infection in Nur Ali's fourteen-month old grandson had developed as a lung infection. Since Ahmad and Iqbal were both absent, the *qaida* had arranged for escorts to get the women and Aftab to the hospital to have his lungs checked and receive treatment. Naser and Yusuf took turns with this. He preferred Yusuf's help only because he had a motorcycle, a popular way to get around in the city. Sher Banu could sit sideways on the back seat, as women did, cradling her baby in one arm while holding onto Yusuf's arm with the other hand.

Before each hospital visit, Nur Ali warned them to be vigilant and remain at the child's side every moment.

"Keep a sharp eye," he warned Sher Banu. "There is always a danger of bad people who roam through hospitals looking to abduct unattended children." The *qaida's* craving to be the resourceful guide, coupled with the agony of helplessness, and alienated by time and space, left him with no close role, and relegated him to his usual monologue lecturing approach. It wasn't what he wanted, but it was the only way he knew to communicate anymore.

When Sher Banu explained to him the process of extracting liquid from the lungs with a needle, her father-in-law warned, "They use dirty needles. You need to insist that they clean the needles thoroughly."

Every call home was highlighted by an update on the child.

"He's okay. He's eating again," reported Nazia to her grandfather. She had listened to enough conversations to understand that appetite was considered an indicator of health.

"What are you all doing?" Nur Ali asked his granddaughter.

"I'm making bread with Mother." Nur Ali could almost smell it.

"What are you cooking for me tonight?" He asked

"Bread and tea."

"That's not enough for me," teased Nur Ali. "Make up a good meat dish. I'm hungry. Where is Bibi?"

"She's washing laundry."

"What? No one does her laundry for her?"

Nur Ali was horrified that Shahgofta's daughters-in-law were not taking better care of their mother-in-law. Her days of labor should have been over by now, even with Naseema gone. But he did not want to impose this worry on the child, and instead prodded her teasingly, "Does your mother hit you?"

"Yes," replied Nazia, matter-of-factly, unable to see the gentleness and twinkle in his eyes. Physical punishment was commonly practiced among Pashtuns. In his mind, Nur Ali could still see his own mother throwing her plastic sandal at him when he stole bread from the basket as a child or was slow to get moving on a chore. The women of his childhood would routinely remove their shoe to raise it or some other object in a threatening gesture of hurling it at him or other children while screaming imprecations. And the children met the threat with dodging and laughter, and accepted it as general behavior. In the mountains of Swat, throwing stones at animals was the method used to keep them in line, whether to shoo a stray dog, or deter a grazing animal from wandering too far from the herd. For some things, raising children was akin to raising animals.

"Why does she hit you?" he asked.

"I don't know" the child answered her grandfather.

"You tell her I said not to hit you. Go tell her right now," Nur Ali ordered Nazia. He laughed, as he and his granddaughter repeated this verbal ritual that was common to many of their conversations.

"Salam alaykum." Shahgofta's voice came on as she took the phone from Nazia.

"Walaykum salam. The girl told me Aftab is doing better. She also told me you are washing laundry. What's going on?"

"He seems to have improved since the operation. But he still doesn't eat, and just lies listless. We're giving him the medicine."

"Take good care of him," urged the *qaida*. He forgot entirely about the laundry. "And don't hesitate to take him back to the doctor. I can cover the expense."

"Did you get the papers from your lawyer yet?" Shahgofta changed the subject.

"No," replied Nur Ali. "He won't give them to me until I have a plane ticket, and I don't have enough money. I saw him the other day. He has all my documents prepared and said I could go as soon as I have a ticket. I'm working on it. He also reminded me that I would never be able to return here. I reminded him that I had no desire to return. We'll be celebrating our reunion in a few short weeks. Tell the kids to be happy and prepare a party. Last night I dreamed I was packing up."

What Nur Ali failed to tell his wife was that he knew for certain that federal agents were surveilling him . They had shown up the morning before just as he was getting off at seven, and taken him in their black SUV to their building downtown for questioning about his son and about his own plans. Through an interpreter, they questioned him with insistence about the money he was sending to Pakistan and alleged it was going to support Taliban. He could only reply that it was all going for family and for holiday distributions. They knew from Nur Ali's lawyer that he had rescinded his petition for asylum and was preparing to leave, and they were satisfied that he was doing it on his own. It was simply a last attempt to obtain information while he was still in their territory.

Shahgofta asked about the phone that Naser had requested.

"I have an iPhone on hold for seven hundred dollars but have not paid for it yet."

"I don't understand," his wife cried out. "Just yesterdayyou said you could not afford it."

"What choice do I have? As *qaida,* I am responsible for everything and everyone in this family. It would eat at me my entire life if I didn't fulfill my son's request from me."

Shahgofta laughed teasingly at her husband.

"By the way," he added, "ask around and see if anyone needs me to bring anything. Ask them all. All I have is the clothes and blanket I left with fifteen years ago, so I can bring over as much as I want."

"I already told you, don't bring anything. Your fifteen-year-old clothes and blanket are useless here. We have new clothes for you. Why bring that old stuff? I just didn't know your size."

"You're welcome, Buddy," Nur Ali addressed a customer in English, then returned to Shahgofta. "You don't know my size?!"

"I haven't seen you in years. How should I know your size?"

"Are my personal belongings still there?"

"Yes."

"How about my watch?"

"No, that I gave to your son. We'll buy whatever you need."

"With what money?" he switched tactics again, "I have no money. I'm just Nur Ali, and I don't have money to buy expensive things. Everyone has spent all my retirement savings. They bought land or paid their expenses, and now they have nothing left to pay me back with. You won't be upset by my beard?"

"Since when is anyone offended by a beard?"

"If you were, I'd have to give you a talking to." He laughed. "You know… life is finally winding down. My days and life of work and exile are nearing an end. That's what life is all about, isn't it? You'll be happy to have me home, won't you?" He arched his back slightly, waiting for her answer, and reached his hand to press the sacrum, easing the dull throb.

"We'll see," Shahgofta said. "You've been saying you're coming home for so long now, I'm not holding my breath ."

"What are you cooking tonight?" Nur Ali asked her.

"Potatoes."

"Keep some aside for me. I am nestled in your heart," he told her in parting.

PAKISTAN NOW

Nur Ali called his brother, Yusuf Ali, to check on his sons' progress with finding work in Qatar. They had landed short-term jobs as truck and bus drivers, but nothing firm, and he was anxious for them to start replacing him as bread winners. The boys were out when he called, but Yusuf Ali was very upset and had bad news to report. Mahmad Ali had returned to Khwaza Khel and knocked down the wall separating their homes, taking over Nur Ali's house and claiming ownership of the entire family compound. As if that wasn't enough, he was also spreading slanderous gossip, saying there was reason to believe that Iqbal's wife was being unfaithful to him, that she was running around Karachi on her own. There was no one left in Khwaza Khel to contest the slander.

A rush of rage and terror passed through the *qaida's* body like none he had felt before. He stood quietly and willed himself to breathe, trying to talk himself out of nonsense. *I must compose myself. By slander, my own brother is driving me out of the village.*

Despite having vowed never to speak to his brother again, despair made Nur Ali call Mahmad Ali to personally vouch for his daughter-in-law. He had to protect her reputation at once. Spurred by visions recalling the stoning of women for allegations of infidelity in his village, his fingers trembled as he pushed the numbers on the phone. He knew that people loved a

255

scandal, thronged in excited anticipation of the event, and didn't seek any evidence beyond the slander launched by an angry relative. If not corrected publicly, such slander would make it impossible for Iqbal to ever return to Khwaza Khel with Sher Banu. It would also make it easier for Mahmad Ali to claim the home.

"You have no right to spread foul untruths about my daughter-in-law. Do you realize she's fighting for her son's health as we speak? Remember that she's your niece as much as she is mine by our mother. Sher Banu is a decent girl. She's done nothing to give anyone reason to doubt her fidelity to my son, your nephew. You are doing this out of spite to me, and you are hurting an innocent, already suffering girl in the process. And you're hurting the boy. You know full well that this kind of slander will force him to divorce or kill his wife. He won't be able to bring her home." Nur Ali swore over the Quran that he was aware of every activity in his house, of every coming and going, and that he had never seen an ounce of devious behavior in Sher Banu. He hung up after speaking his mind, not waiting for a reply.

When Nur Ali called Sardar Ali to report his call to their brother, he added that Mahmad Ali just wanted to assure his unquestioned ownership of the family home, and that he could only do so by harming the *qaida*'s reputation, as well as that of his family. What easier way than to slander his foe's daughter-in-law?

"It's on account of people like him," Nur Ali told his brother, "that our country is Muslim in name only. They say our government is no longer even Muslim. Calling yourself Muslim does not make you a Muslim, but a hypocrite. Do you remember our father's teachings about hypocrisy? He called it the lowest and worst of crimes. Our country is run by hypocrites. Islam has become an enemy to Muslim people like you and me, like the mother of the mullah of Deolai, washed away by the flood. Like the widow from our village whose only son disappeared, was jailed, and then returned as a corpse to be buried. People who continue to suffer the blows that Allah pounds us with will be oppressed by the government that calls itself Muslim. Our brother represents what our country has become."

Sardar Ali agreed. He expressed sympathy and added that he would talk with Mahmad Ali. Then he asked Nur Ali how his case was coming along with the US.

"I signed papers requesting to rescind my request for asylum," Nur Ali explained. "It's no longer about the money. What can money mean to a man who is not content? Without my wife and family, what is life worth? I know I may be returning to my death, that I'm possibly facing a death sentence. But I no longer have a choice." His eyes shot down to see his free hand furiously scratching his arm. When had he become so unaware of this physical ailment? He willed himself to stop, despite the fierce itching, and set his hand on the counter.

"You are like the people who jump from windows when the building is on fire," Sardar Ali said sadly. "Don't despair, brother. We are here and will help you in any way possible. You have worked hard and given everything you earned to help others. I understand you feel defeated, but Allah is on your side, and will take care of you." Somewhat comforted by his brother's words, Nur Ali said goodbye.

He smoothed his beard with his free hand, calming himself for a moment before calling Yusuf Ali back to ask his brother to investigate getting him a transit visa so he could visit his sons in Qatar on his way home. Sobbing now, choking on his words, he added that they were all he had left. He had already been told that transit visas were not being issued, and that he would not be able to leave the airport for any duration. "I'll look into it," Yusuf Ali said, "it might be expensive, but I'll make inquiries and let you know." They said goodbye.

It was not long before the phone rang again.

PAKISTAN NOW

"Hello, 7-Eleven." Nur Ali picked up, knowing that any call at that hour was inevitably for him. He heard Bacha Gul's voice.

"Salam alaykum." The two friends liked to talk around two o'clock, after things slowed down slightly, and they had time to kill. "You alone tonight?"

"Yes, the other guy left at midnight. And my bosses are gone."

"Where are they?" asked Bacha Gul.

"They're seven hours away by plane." They had gone to California and had explained it in these terms to Nur Ali: "It's like ten times from Swat to Karachi." Nur Ali continued, "They're good people. Who else would give an old man a job?"

"You're not that old!" retorted Bacha Gul.

"I'm all white, and I've sworn never to put scissors to my beard again."

"Anyway, guess who happened into my store earlier. You remember Rahman, that young Afghan kid who grew up here, and was having family problems a while ago?"

"Oh, him," started Nur Ali. "He's never even been there. What does he understand of hostility, of village talk, or of what's important to us? Don't even bother talking to him. He says he doesn't understand what we talk about, anyway. Folks who have never lived there can't relate to the way we talk. Pashtuns are always hostile toward one another, even among us exiles. Look at Haji Sahib's sons who came here and never offered me a penny, gift, or anything in thanks for helping them get set up. And my cousin who borrowed money and never paid anything back. Everyone here is cutthroat and cheating each other. No community. We all just struggle for ourselves."

"Well," Bacha Gul steered the conversation back to Rahman and his Moroccan wife. "He seems to understand our principles that govern lack of privacy and self. He was on the phone with his wife, warning her to be kind to his visiting parents who were threatening to leave because the house was so messy. She tried claiming that the house was her private property, and he argued with her that nothing was private. With us Pashtuns, nothing is completely private. You know you can't even eat something in public without having to share it with everyone. And the idea of privacy in your home! Where did she get that one? Maybe in Morocco!"

The two men, each in their respective 7-Eleven, resumed as always, their favorite pastime with each other, sharing stories of Pashtuns, both at home and in exile. Bacha Gul had no issues tonight with his register, credit card scanner, or lottery tickets, which Nur Ali so often helped him with. He had no medical issues for Nur Ali to advise him on with home remedies, so they just talked and exchanged gossip.

"Oh, here's a good one for you." It was Nur Ali's turn to provide a piece of news. "You know Asok Jan from Damghar? His father had taken a second wife along with the first, you know. When his father died recently, he left his house and three shops to his second wife and children. Asok Jan's own mother received nothing, even though she'd been married to the man all those years. No one gives a damn about anyone anymore."

"Yes," added Bacha Gul. "I heard that when Asok Jan went home for his father's funeral after years of working here, he sat his mother down, who was expecting a bundle of money, and told her he was broke, and that she should be grateful he hadn't brought home any foreign debts."

Nur' Ali's scratching hand reached for his beard instead, as he fleetingly wondered whether it belonged to a world he had lost. "Yeah," he conceded, "it's not what people make it out to be, coming here to work, or even going to the Gulf countries. There are uneducated Pashtuns all over this city, too poor to survive, and begging for financial assistance at the mosques. I discourage all my relatives who want to come here for work. It's not a place for us."

It was Bacha Gul's turn. "And the ones who bring their wives are the worst off. The men work around the clock while the women stay locked in cold empty rooms with nothing to do or eat. Moambar's wife lost her mind, she was so homesick for her parents and family, and he just left her there day after day. I think he was disgusted with her."

"Once you're here," continued Nur Ali, "it's hard to leave again. You put all this effort out to come here, and then realize you're stuck and can't go home. Pashtuns talk about going home all the time, but only a few ever do. I have all these gifts stashed away to send home with people, but no one ever leaves for Pakistan anymore."

Although he had discussed his return home with relatives, Nur Ali had not spoken about it with any of the exiled community. When he was ready, he planned simply to ask Mir Zaman, the taxi driver, to get him to the airport.

Later that night, concluding a discussion about inflation and unemployment, Bacha Gul said that people back home were selling their own children to scrape by. "Saudis offer a good price for girls from Swat. They like them because our girls are strong workers, accustomed to a simple life. No one can get loans. They cheat and steal from their own families now. Selling daughters is a convenient solution."

"Don't talk to me about that," said Nur Ali, disturbed by the topic. "Stay in touch with your own family. That's all we have left now. It's what keeps us going each day, what keeps us alive." He realized he was gripping his beard tightly, and recalled the dream had that left him with a hairless face.

PAKISTAN NOW

"Salam alaykum," Nur Ali's voice was hard, anxious, and his brow furrowed.

"Walaykum salam," replied Shahgofta in a sleepy voice.

"Were you asleep?"

"No," she replied. "Just lying down."

"How is the child?" It was the second time tonight Nur Ali was calling to inquire after his grandson Aftab, whose condition had worsened.

"He seems to be improving," she replied. "He drank from his mother's breast today."

"That's good. Don't let anything happen to my baby grandson until I get home. You take care of him."

"One, thirty-six," Nur Ali interrupted their conversation to speak English to a customer buying a cup of coffee, and then returned. "People here drink coffee like we drink tea. It's their own thing. I've tried it a few times, but I don't like it. How is the heat?" Karachi could be insufferably hot in the summer, and the power outages left people without even fans.

"It's bearable. How about where you are? Is it very hot?"

"Here," described Nur Ali, pressing his hand into his lower back, "you never feel hot or cold. Allah made that kind of deal for this land. But this country cannot exist without electricity for even a minute. If it's the slightest bit warm, they run the air conditioning. And at the first hint of cold, they run the heat. You never feel either one."

"Can you eat in the store?" questioned Shahgofta.

"No, I don't get anything here. It's overpriced, and I can find everything cheaper in other stores. Most people don't shop in this store."

"Why don't you lower your prices?"

"Company prices are fixed," explained Nur Ali, who had given up engaging in this conversation with his bosses some time ago.

"Where do you shop?" she asked

"I've told you many times…at the Indian store. They have halal meats and everything we eat: lentils, spices, rice, tea. They even carry henna, but no *naswar*. And the Afghan store has lots of nuts and fruit, both dried and fresh. Their prices are good too."

"Speaking of prices," Shahgofta began rattling a long list of food prices, specifically of meats. The religious holiday was approaching, in commemoration of Abraham's sacrifice of his son, and Muslims throughout the world were carving out budgets for the purchase of animals to sacrifice, distribute, and eat on the holiday. From a single chicken to multiple cows and buffalo, it all depended on one's wealth and budget. This year, Shahgofta and Nur Ali's cousin, who lived in the same building and helped them out, would jointly buy a goat for the sacrifice.

"We'll need money," Shahgofta announced the obvious.

"You and everyone else," responded Nur Ali, managing to laugh, although he was now scratching his arm and feeling the familiar knot swell in his stomach.

"Yes, well, everyone always needs money. Just last night Naser was questioning how many days were left till your next pay day."

As Nur Ali had pulled back from sending money to family members, their cries grew stronger, and he spoke to his wife about his changing position. "The women are all upset because they have no money. Well, it's up to their husbands to send them money now. It's up to their sons. During all my years of exile, my earnings have gone to cover others' needs, and nothing is left for me. My cousins and in-laws called me consistently to ask about me when they needed money. Now that they know I need it and can no longer dish it out, I never hear from them anymore. It's like you. I always call you. What if I told you you had to call me?"

"I don't have the money to call you," answered Shahgofta.

"And why not? You have two adult sons. Have they contributed anything toward the holiday sacrifice?"

Shahgofta remained silent, reminded that her sons were slow to take up their role of breadwinner for the family.

"I'm a Muslim and a Pashtun. Don't I know everything?" exclaimed Nur Ali, implying that he knew very well what his sons did and did not send home. It was his stock response to the obvious but inevitable.

"Okay, I'll call you tomorrow."

PAKISTAN NOW

"Hello, 7-Eleven." It was just after midnight, still early to be getting calls from home, and Nur Ali was not expecting this one.

"Walaykum salam, Lala, how are you? Is everything okay?"

"Time passes by, and I'm passing my time. How are you?"

"I'm fine," said the voice. But I'm afraid I have some bad news for you."

"Who is this?" Nur Ali did not recognize Sardar Ali's voice.

"It's me, your brother. I'm calling about Aftab. He didn't make it. He died last night," Sardar Ali announced slowly.

"Allah! Just last night they told me he was better, and that he had fed from his mother's breast!" cried Nur Ali.

"Yes, but he started coughing again in the middle of the night, and then he couldn't breathe. He was gasping for air and choking. Yusuf took Sher Banu and the child on the motorcycle from one clinic and hospital to another all night, but there was nothing they could do."

Nur Ali was too stunned by the news to respond. He hung up quietly. He had been actively involved over the past two weeks in orchestrating hospital visits and calling continually for updates and advising household members on what to do. Now nothing. At one point, amid a long-winded diatribe to the family, he had claimed, "I may be old and finished, but even from afar, I'm still the family *qaida..*" He had called two to three times a night to check on the child and offer advice, and just last night Sher Banu had reported that Aftab seemed to be improving. What was a *qaida* supposed to do now?

No longer able to deny his shattered financial dreams or his alienated family, the sudden death of his grandson had brought him crashing down to a state of blind despair, in which he could not focus beyond getting home.

Within minutes, he regathered his wits sufficiently to push the numbers on the phone with trembling fingers and call Shahgofta. The two of them sobbed and wailed together, lamenting the loss of their grandson. His free hand scratched his arm almost to blood. "This is Allah's doing," he tried to console his wife, "there was nothing we could do. We must endure with patience what He gives us. But," he sobbed, "the child's father was not even there, and he will live to mourn that until he dies."

When they caught their breath and could talk, she reported the painful last night of Aftab's life, after which they shared some better memories.

"Remember when we all cried with joy at his birth, and Iqbal said he looked like a radiant sun in the midst of the horrible floods and destruction?" Nur Ali said.

"I approved that name right away," she replied.

Nur Ali had never physically seen Aftab, nor any of his grandchildren for that matter, and knew them from their voices only. They were all dear to him, but this boy, born of his favorite son and daughter-in-law, had become a part of him. The *qaida* had assumed a parental role with both Sher Banu and Aftab.

He asked how Sher Banu was doing.

"She is too grief-stricken and beside herself to speak with anyone," Shahgofta explained. "The apartment is already filled with wailing women who have come for condolences." Shahgofta also reported that the local mullah had said he himself would bathe and prepare the body, seeing as there were no immediate adult male relatives, and the mother was not of sound enough mind to function beyond her grief.

When Nur Ali called his brother back to offer assistance with funeral arrangements, Sardar Ali asked his brother to stop calling them so frequently, to free up the lines for other condolence callers. He also advised giving Sher Banu a few days to compose herself. He reassured Nur Ali that both Iqbal and Ahmad were alright and had taken a few days off to remain at home.

"I've purchased a ticket home,"Nur Ali announced .

"That's good. Will you stop to see your boys in Qatar on the way?"

"That child died with no father, no grandfather, no uncles, and no brothers to take care of him. Maybe I can move up my departure date and get back in time to carry his body to Khwaza Khel for burial and arrange his funeral."

"No, don't rush for that," Sardar Ali advised. "Yusuf has already made all the necessary arrangements. He'll take care of everything, and I'm heading down there too."

"Maybe this was all a result of Mahmad Ali's evil eye toward me," Nur Ali suggested bitterly. "Our brother wished bad things for me and my family ever since we broke up over our family home."

"Maybe," responded Sardar Ali, unable to refute the suggestion and knowing exactly what his brother was implying. The destructive powers of the evil eye were at work. "But the child wore a talisman, didn't he?"

"Of course! We bought it from the mullah in Karachi. He should have been protected." Nur Ali recalled lecturing his children about getting a talisman right after the child was born to protect him from giving or receiving the evil eye. He had even suggested scarring Aftab so as not to attract envy, but Iqbal had protested at the extreme measure.

They said goodbye to free the line in Karachi.

A strange stillness hung over the store. It was empty and quiet. The *qaida* leaned his elbows on the counter and wept bitterly into his hands. He questioned his existence and failure to lead his clan. His plan to earn for his family and retirement had failed. He had toiled for years, alienated from family and home, living in utter isolation both in America and from home, had provided for all his family's needs, and yet here he felt eviscerated with nothing left for himself. His future was wholly uncertain and unknown.

But he needed to compose himself, yet again, for just before his shift was over, two federal agents arrived at the store to take Nur Ali in for questioning about his situation. He went with them, sat demurely and answered all their questions in a voice they could barely hear. The interpreter offered tea and cookies, but he declined both. During the questioning, with head drooped, Nur Ali confirmed to them that he had bought a ticket back to

Pakistan. Only louder than a whisper, he added that his grandson had just died, and he was going home.

They were pleased to hear this, that they themselves did not have to take action to deport him, and the rest of the interview wrapped up quickly. They insisted on escorting Nur Ali to the airport when he left, to witness his departure from the country.

"You are obliged to fly directly to Pakistan," one of the officers added. "You won't be permitted to stop in Qatar."

They also assumed that Pakistani authorities would pick Nur Ali up as soon as he deplaned in Karachi, but it was no longer their responsibility to inform him.

Nur Ali called again for an update from Shahgofta on who had called for condolences. He also questioned in detail who had or was crying and lamenting. These formal laments, gut-wrenching chants of agony and sorrow, were a clear sign of closeness and loyalty among Pashtun women. Though the Taliban had banned them, they were so deeply rooted in local tradition that they were not likely to be erased. It was expected that the deceased's mother, wife, daughters, or sisters would be mad with grief and ailment to the point of not being able to speak; it was three days before Sher Banu was able to address her father-in-law on the phone, and her voice was deep and raspy from days of wailing and lamenting.

"Oh, *Qaidada*," she sobbed. "He was so white and pure, so innocent. You never got to see him!"

Nur Ali let her lament to him, and then attempted to console her. "Be strong, my child. Pray for patience." He had learned to recite these formulas from his father at home. And he recalled them also from numerous occasions as a child when he had accompanied his mother to laments.

"Didn't the Prophet's own son die? It is Allah's will. He doesn't give people more than they need or can endure. He will give you more children. You must let this one go." Next, he spoke with each family member there, and then he instructed them to console Sher Banu.

When Nur Ali spoke with Yusuf, his nephew told him that he had taken care of everything for the funeral, and that the *qaida* need not move up his reservation.

After hanging up, Nur Ali was able to call Iqbal in Qatar, so that father and son could also commiserate.

"It was Allah's will, my son," he recited the formulas in an attempt to convince either or both of them as the two cried together. "He does this to test our patience. You'll have more children."

Driven by an overpoweringly visceral need to be home, Nur Ali removed all the cash he had left from the safe in the back room, and called his friend, Matthew, to help him get his ticket. He then brought his ticket to his attorney and received his passport and papers, and finally he called Mir Zaman to ask if he would help him get to the airport for his flight home. He also had to notify the authorities of his travel plans, so they could see him off. He had not said a word at the store, for fear they would cut his hours before he was ready to quit. Leaving enough cash on the table in his house to cover what was left of his rent and portion of food, without a word Nur Ali left his life as the 7-Eleven night-shift worker, departed from his lonely life of exile, and headed home. Even when his flight landed for refueling in Qatar, he remained unmoved by the thought that his sons were there.

As his Qatar Airways flight took off down the runway toward Pakistan, the passenger next to him asked where he was headed. For the weary Nur Ali, a single word summed it up.

"Home."

NOTES

*Yusuf Khan aw Bibi Sher Banu, chapbook written by Ali Heydar Joshi and published by Rahman Gul Publisher, Qissa Khwani, Peshawar. Sung by Wahid Gul and mass produced on cassettes in local markets in north-western Pakistan. Translated into French by Benedicte Grima Johnson, Les contes legendaires Pashtun: Analyse et traduction de cassettes commercialisees. (p.97-120).

** Although there exist published collections of *tappas*, or couplets, the three appearing here are not recorded. I collected hundreds of these during field work, noting many of them down or committing them to memory. They are a form of folk poetry, often made up on the spot.